FALLING FOR A YOUNG

King

A NOVEL BY

VIVIAN BLUE

Royalty Publishing House is now accepting manuscripts from aspiring or experienced urban romance authors!

WHAT MAY PLACE YOU ABOVE THE REST:

Heroes who are the ultimate book bae: strong-willed, maybe a little rough around the edges but willing to risk it all for the woman he loves.

Heroines who are the ultimate match: the girl next door type, not perfect - has her faults but is still a decent person. One who is willing to risk it all for the man she loves.

The rest is up to you! Just be creative, think out of the box, keep it sexy and intriguing!

If you'd like to join the Royal family, send us the first 15K words (60 pages) of your completed manuscript to submissions@royaltypublishinghouse.com

Get LiT with our LiT eReading App!

I would like to dedicate this release to the love of my life,
William Maurice Kemper, aka Kamose Shabaka Shakur.
To know love is to know pain.
I will love you always and forever!!

ONE

Elizabeth "Izzy" James—The Stylist to Celebrities, Professionals, and Socialites

---

"WHY DID you leave so early this morning, Izzy? You normally stay and cook breakfast for us, and I had my mouth set on an omelet but had to settle on Cheerios," said Craig, complaining as usual.

"You know I had that photoshoot to do this morning at five o'clock," I explained, but truth be told, I left that ass early this morning because our session last night was horrible. I guess he thought he was doing something since his dick managed to stay hard for ten minutes instead of six. This dude was forty-four years old, and he called himself fucking me and a twenty-one-year-old model. Hell, he didn't have enough stamina for me, so how in the hell was he going to add someone else to the party?

"I know your ass was tired because I wore that thang out," Craig bragged.

"I didn't enjoy that shit. It would have been a better time if you would have sucked me up and used the vibrator to get me off. Your mediocre sex is really starting to get boring."

"You're joking, right?" Craig asked, trying to play it off. "You know I knocks you down properly, so don't start with that bullshit, Izzy."

"You're the one who started it Craig. I was trying to spare your little feelings, and I've been telling you this for the past few months."

"I can't help it if *your* sex is boring. I have the most amazing sex with a twenty-one-year-old, and I never hear her complain."

See, that was the shit that I was talking about. He'd always throw up in my face the fact that he was fucking a child. I bet if I had a twenty-something year old fucking me, I would be a happy camper too. Yoshi don't give a damn about whether or not his dick was good as long as he was paying her rent, taking her shopping and on vacations, and making sure she went out in public to be seen by the who's who in the entertainment industry. That bitch was perfectly fine with the six-minute man.

"You know what, Craig? Fuck you for real. You're not doing me any favors you know. I can play with my own coochie and actually achieve an orgasm," I spat angrily at him.

"Well, next time that's what your ass is going to have to do when your pussy gets wet, Izzy! I'm putting you on restriction."

"Whatever, Craig," I said, hanging up on him. My assistant, Jack, walked into my office with a folder in his hand and sat it on my desk. It was my next assignment, and I was looking forward to throwing myself into my work. My relationship with Craig wasn't going anywhere, but I owed him for helping with my success, and I felt a bit indebted to him. We had a mutual agreement to be non-exclusive because he's not ready for a committed relationship. I fell for the shit four years ago and thought maybe he would change his mind, but boy was I wrong. I'd suffered through numerous bad situations with him and the other hoes that he's dealt with. I even had to deal with a case of gonorrhea where he swore that it must have come from me having a yeast infection. Now, ain't that a bitch!

"I think you're going to enjoy this assignment," Jack said, giggling. "You're dressing Duchess McDaniel for her photoshoot for *California Living*. She's one of the prominent housewives of Pasadena and her husband is—"

"The CEO of Linx Technologies," I finished, reading it from the file. "It says here that he's one of the fifth richest men in the United States, which I wouldn't have known that information if I hadn't read it. The sheet goes on to say that Duchess likes to garden and feed the homeless. She's a part of the board at a shelter, and she has a degree in elementary education."

Shuffling through the papers in the folder, I came across a family photo. Staring at it for a moment made me realize that I knew two of the people in the picture and happened to be good friends with them.

"This is Athlon," I said, pointing to her. "Do you remember me doing a photoshoot for her jewelry collection?" Jack came around my desk and stared at the photo over my shoulder for a second, but his attention was diverted to someone else.

"Did you see this scrumptious man standing next to Duchess with those piercing green eyes and long dreadlocks?" Jack questioned, snatching the picture out of my hand. "I'd eat him right up in that garden where Duchess loves to prune her roses."

"Sounds like you're the one who wants to be pruned," I said jokingly, taking the photo out of Jack's hand. Staring at it, I didn't notice the handsome young man, but now that Jack brought him to my attention, I couldn't take my eyes off of him.

"You know Duchess is Chester's second wife. He was having an affair with her while we were in college. Evelyn, his first wife, found out about Duchess and left his ass high and dry with the kids. He had two older children; Chess right here is who I went college with," I explained pointing to him. "He must be the baby that came along and broke up the first marriage."

"You know all of those people's business," Jack said, rolling his eyes. "I hope you don't be telling people none of mine when you be talking about me." I looked at Jack like he had shit on his face.

"Why would you think that I would discuss you with anyone? I don't even like you that much. When we're away from each other I cherish that time alone." Jack turned his lips up at me, smirking.

"Guuuurl, you funny," he said, walking over to the door. "You better eat something because we have a long day ahead of us. You got three clients coming in for fittings, and you have to do a sheet for Ms. Duchess."

Rolling my eyes at Jack was a normal occurrence several times a day, and this time was no different.

"Who scheduled three fittings for one day?" I questioned, frowning.

"You did, dear because you wanted to clear your calendar for the weekend," Jack replied before prancing out of my office. It may have seemed like I didn't really like my assistant, but in actuality, Jack was my best friend. He made sure I ate and took my medication, so my diabetes was under control. I managed to lose enough weight to get off of insulin, but it was an ongoing battle to make sure I stayed off of it for the rest of my life. My eating habits had become excellent, but my weakness for alcohol and wine was the vice that was going to kill me.

FEELING TIRED, the only thing I wanted to do when I got home was heat up my dinner and have a few glasses of wine. Entering my condo, I locked the door behind me before dragging myself up the steps and bypassing the kitchen. I decided to get out of these clothes to get the day off of me, and a shower would definitely do the job.

Somehow. my body managed to relax, even though I was thinking about that asshole, Craig. He pissed me off by always throwing Yoshi up in my face. The bitch wasn't even Japanese, and her family was from Brooklyn. I guess they were Super Mario Brothers fans, and that's how she got her name. Don't call me a hater. I thought that she was really cute. I was not an ugly chick, so I didn't have any reason to diss the next woman. Even though Craig tried to say that I was jealous of Yoshi, the only thing I was envious about was her melanin-rich skin. I wanted to be chocolate like that, but my skin was a nice caramel color like my mother, but my face is the spitting image of my father. My almond shaped eyes, high cheekbones, and full lips come from my gram. We were named after the queen of England because her mother was obsessed with the woman. She was the person who inspired my love for fashion and pearl necklaces. She bought me my first set when I was five years old and taught me how to dress. I still had all the necklaces to this day along with several pairs of hers that she passed down to me. Those were the only sentimental things that left with me when we decided to leave St. Louis.

My brother Kevin and I moved out to California eleven years ago. He was chasing after this girl he swore that he was in love with. We shared a shitty apartment in Chinatown until we were able to move into another shitty spot in East Hollywood. I was substitute teaching at a private school during the day and working as an assistant to his chick at night.

Pusilla had landed a gig being a high-priced escort, and she left my brother in pursuit of bigger fish. She always liked the way I dressed and did my hair, so she would pay me three hundred dollars a week to do her hair and makeup. Also, Pusilla would pay me to go shopping for her to pick out her outfits for her dates. That's how I met Craig. She introduced me to him. By the time we became friends, I was already dressing several of the girls at the escort business, and her boss wanted to hire me to dress his entire staff of high priced hoes. However, Craig intervened and introduced me to a publicist that had a few A-List celebrity friends who he convinced to give me a shot. The rest was history, and here I was Izzy James, the stylist to celebrities, professionals, and socialites.

Strolling down the steps to the kitchen, my stomach started growling. There was a note stuck to the refrigerator from my house-keeper telling me not to drink an entire bottle of wine, but I was not paying her ass any attention. She needed to mind her own business, and my house better had been spotless, or else there was going to be a note left for her ass in the morning.

I grabbed a bottle of white wine off the top shelf and yanked the note down. Also, I picked up my large container of food and shut the door behind me. The one thing that was a guarantee was that my meal would be healthy. My housekeeper Jen was the person who became very proactive with my eating habits when I got sick. She used to make me drink those nasty smoothies that had all the green vegetables in it and a lemon. What the hell was a lemon going to do when you're mixing it with broccoli, cucumbers, and collard greens? I damn near threw up every time I drank that nasty shit, but it helped me get better. I lost over fifty pounds and dropped down several dress sizes going from a sixteen to a size eight, depending on the quality of the clothing. A bitch was Rainbowed out until the real coin came in, and designers started throwing their clothes to me to wear. I loved my career, and I planned on going all the way to fashion week with my own line someday. The grind is relentless, and I knew my chance was going to come soon enough.

My food was in the microwave, so I popped the cork out of the wine. I grabbed the biggest goblet that was in my cabinet and poured myself a tall glass of Chardonnay. That shit was sixty dollars a bottle, but it was good as hell and what was needed to do my homework on Duchess McDaniel. I was sure she was going to be a diva, but who names their little black daughter "Duchess" anyway? That was something you name a pet.

The microwave beeped, and I made my way over to it. The toaster oven does a better job of heating up food, but I was feeling impatient and hungry. My blood sugar was dropping a little, and the last thing I needed was to get sick.

Taking my food out and placing it on the counter I stirred it up and reached for my glass of wine while pushing my food over to my laptop. It was time to Google Duchess.

I remembered knowing her stepson and his wife, so I mentally made a to email Athlon so that maybe we could meet for lunch. This was going to be an interesting experience, but I was up for the challenge.

TWO

Izzy

────────

THE NEXT MORNING, I woke up to the sound of my phone ringing off the hook. I had fallen asleep at the counter and didn't make it up to my bed last night. A discovery was made that Duchess McDaniel, formally known as Duchess Crest, was the daughter of Samuel Crest, a major player from Long Beach. I remember going out and partying with him in my early twenties. He was my friend Ash's sugar daddy, and he used to foot the bill for all of us. If we were going out on the town, he would pay for all of us an outfit. His wife had found out about Ash and ran her out of town.

My phone went off again, and I looked down at it, feeling quite annoyed. It was Jack calling for the millionth time, and my eyes rolled up in my head. I was already tired of him, and we hadn't even spoken yet.

"Hello," I mumbled, sounding tired, yawning in his ear.

"Where the hell are you?" Jack snapped at me. "Your appointment is here, and you're ten minutes late."

"Shit! I know it's not ten o'clock already. Boy! Here I come," I said, jumping up from my stool. Rushing up the steps made me think about how it's a good thing that I had taken a shower last night because all I had to do was wash my face, vital parts, brush my teeth, put on my clothes, and I was out of there. My condo was in the city and not that far from my studio located in Downtown LA, so I could take an Uber and get there in no time.

"Order my Uber, and I'll be there in twenty minutes," I said into the phone and hung up. It was going to be a crazy day just by how my morning started.

"IT'S nice of you to finally join us. We've been waiting for you for almost an hour," said Gloria Palmer, the editor I was doing the favor for. She had been a huge supporter of my career, and every so often, I'd style someone for her magazine.

"I'm so sorry, Gloria. It was a long night, and I overslept." I placed my bag and phone on my desk, pulled out my laptop and booted it up while everyone was staring at me. Next, I pulled out my notebook to take notes because the woman sitting in front of me looked like high maintenance.

"Let me introduce everyone to you," Gloria said, trying to get things rolling. "This is Duchess McDaniel and her son, Kingdom McDaniel."

"It's nice to meet you all," I uttered pleasantly. They both were staring at me like I had tissue hanging from up under my dress. I grabbed the first thing in sight that was hanging in my closet, and it just so happened to be a green tube dress that stopped just above my knees, and I paired it with a yellow blazer and matching yellow pumps to complete the look. My hair was in a bright red, thirty-six-inch wrap with Chinese bangs. I didn't have time to flat iron it, but it still had some flow to it.

"Again, I would like to apologize for my tardiness. It was very unprofessional for me to leave you all waiting, but I guess the few glasses of wine I had last night must have crept up on me." Kingdom was staring at me with his piercing green eyes, and I could feel the hairs on the back of my neck stand up.

"It's all right, Izzy, as long as it doesn't happen again," Duchess replied in a kind voice. "King has an engagement at noon, and this was the only time that I could get to spend with him. He's a senior at UCLA and will be graduating summa cum laude in six months with a degree in information systems."

"That's amazing," I babbled. I wanted to say that his face was amazing, but that would have been totally inappropriate.

"I minor in photography as well," Kingdom added. "I wanted to be a photojournalist, but my mother convinced me to follow in my father's footsteps."

"That's amazing," came out again as my eyes lustfully gazed at him. Jack slid me a note and tapped me on the arm. The note said *Bitch snap out of it! Yes, he's fine, but you don't have to drool all over the table. Close your mouth!*

I felt so embarrassed. Looking up at Kingdom, he was still staring me down. It was obvious, but he should've been paying attention to me just like everyone else in the room.

"Do you always say 'amazing' when people tell you things?" Kingdom asked curiously. "I mean, I think it's cute, but I'm sure you can come up with other words."

"King, don't be rude," Duchess, corrected him. "I'm sure Izzy is tired after her long night of drinking. I mean, at your age, you need to be conscious of how much alcohol you consume."

Who is this bitch talking about? Is she throwing shade and she's way older than me? I mean how rude is that shit?

"I'm only thirty-three years old. I heard that these are my prime years. I understand that you're forty-four——"

"I'm forty-five... just had a birthday a few months ago," Duchess corrected me. "My son is twenty-two, and I was his age when he was conceived."

"I went to college with your stepson and daughter-in-law. I know them very well, and I've worked on a few campaigns with Athlon. Her jewelry designs are dope."

"That's one of her pieces you're wearing," Kingdom mentioned, pointing to my necklace. I touched it, smiling at him.

"As a matter of fact, it is. This is one of my favorite pieces because of the multi-colored bead pattern," I uttered for some reason. I loved discussing fashion and all types of randomness that dealt with it.

"I like the way it blends with your whole motif," Kingdom said, staring intensely at me. "You wear that septum piercing really well. It makes you look tribal and sexy with that red hair and lipstick you're sporting."

"Kingdom, sweetie," Duchess said, touching his hand. "Is it almost time for your appointment?" He looked down at his watch then over at her.

"Damn," he replied, diverting his eye contact back over to me.

Shit, he was making my spot wet the way he was looking at me like that. I wanted to jump across the table and shove my tongue down his throat, but his mother would probably stop me. It felt like he was flirting with me, but wasn't that what all twenty-somethings did when they were in the presence of a beautiful woman? *Snap out of it!*

"I'll gather some ideas so that I can run them by you in the next few days. It was a pleasure meeting the both of you, and Duchess, I look forward to working with you."

"It was nice to finally meet you, and I'm looking forward to our conversations about the shoot," Duchess said, getting up from her chair. Kingdom stood up as well, stretching his body. The straight leg jeans he was wearing fit snugly in the thigh area, and his bulge caught the eye of both Jack and I. Jack elbowed me, covering his mouth while I just stared in admiration.

"Kingdom, where are your manners?" said Duchess authoritatively, and he looked at her and frowned.

"It was nice meeting you, Izzy. I look forward to seeing you again," Kingdom rambled in a seductive tone. The hairs on the back of my neck stood up again, and a pleasant smile came across my face.

"It was nice meeting you too, Kingdom," I managed to get out. He licked his lips and smiled at me, and I damn near came on myself.

"Call me, King," he replied with a serious expression on his face. That name is fitting because that boy knew he was fine, and for the record, I really thought he was flirting with me. The stretch was definitely intentional so that his print showed, and then he just licked his juicy lips to get them all wet and shit. I was going to have to go up to my office and pull out my bullet.

Jack showed Duchess and Kingdom out while Gloria hung back for minute. We weren't able to discuss all the details of the shoot, but that was something Gloria and I could work out without Duchess being present.

"She's interesting," I said sarcastically to Gloria.

"You know how we do when we arrive," Gloria replied, laughing.

"She didn't arrive when she married Chester," I said confidently. "Duchess's daddy is named Samuel Crest. He was a big player out in Long Beach and had a bunch of businesses and properties around the city. I had a friend that used to date him when we were young, and he took good care of her."

"That's interesting. Her father was a sugar daddy? She didn't mention growing up privileged. Come to think about it, she didn't really talk about her parents at all. The only thing she wanted to talk about was Kingdom with his cute self and her husband," Gloria recalled.

"Calling that young man cute is an insult. That boy is fine, and I would drink his bath water if he was old enough," I admitted with no shame. Gloria had known me long enough to know this about me.

"He was really checking you out. You saw how he was staring at you," Gloria mentioned passively.

"How about I felt it," I replied dramatically, putting my hand against my chest. "Oh my God, to be young again so I could have just a little taste of that rice crispy treat."

"Did you just refer to him as a rice crispy treat?" Gloria asked, looking at me questionably with a smirk on her face.

"I did, and I don't know where that came from, but I bet he knows how to make that dick snap, crackle, and pop!" We both looked at each other and laughed hysterically.

We continued to talk for several more minutes and agreed to

meet up in a few days for lunch. We were walking out when we ran into Duchess and Kingdom again. I thought that they had left, but I guess I was mistaken. Gloria bid us farewell, showing herself out, and I was left alone with the socialite and her fine ass son. The only thing I kept saying to myself was "don't look at his crotch."

"I'm sorry... did you forget something?" I asked with a clueless expression on my face.

"No, your assistant went to get a bottled water for me," Duchess explained.

"Ma, don't forget to tell her about dinner," Kingdom whispered to her.

"Oh... that's right," Duchess said, looking back at Kingdom uncomfortably. "I would like to invite you to a dinner party at our house tomorrow."

Kingdom lifted his eyebrows at me and blew a kiss. My eyes widened by themselves, and I placed both my hands up to my eyes wiping them. *Is Ashton Kutcher going to jump out soon?*

"Thank you for the invitation," I replied coyly. "I'll have to check my schedule to see if tomorrow night is open."

"You don't have anything on your schedule," Jack said, walking up behind me. Glancing over my shoulder at him, my face felt flushed.

"Guess I'll be coming to your house for dinner," I said, flashing a fake smile.

"Uh unh..." Kingdom said, frowning. "Don't ever smile like that again."

His comment made me instantly stop and stare at him like a deer in headlights. I'd never felt nervous around a man before, but there was something about this young man that did something to me. *Stay in your place, little boy,* my brain wanted me to say, but instead, I looked at him strangely.

"You don't like my smile?"

"I didn't say that, but I don't like that one," King replied. "That wasn't natural, and it made you look phony."

"I think you've said plenty, King. You've insulted Izzy enough for one day," Duchess said, cutting into our conversation. "I will email you my address, and I hope you can attend."

"I hope you can make it too," King added with a smirk on his face.

"We'll see," I replied coyly. However, that dinner would be avoided like the plague because King made me feel uneasy. There was something about him that did something to me, and I didn't know if I liked it.

THREE

Kingdom "King" McDaniel

MY MAMA HAD me late for my bi-weekly pussy appointment. That bad boy was penciled in on my calendar, and I didn't miss it for nothing in the world. The chick was late to meet with us, but Izzy was beautiful and didn't look like she was thirty-three. Older women did it for me, and maybe it was because I was a mama's boy.

My mother spoiled me rotten, and I had older siblings that shared in on it as well. My maternal grandfather was a major part of my life, and I got my game for the ladies from Pops. He told me, "Grandson, there are only three things to remember about a woman. You're going to have to learn how to sex her well and eat good snatch because that's the only way to keep a woman happy, and showering her with gifts is a way to maintain the other two. The money part won't be a problem, but I'm going to teach you how to do the other key things well."

I was only ten years old when he told me that, but for some reason, it stuck with me all my life. Pops was a muthafucka, and he made no apologizes for it. He played professional basketball and did some tampering around in the streets. Pops was really known as a ladies' man, and there was a myth that he slept with over six hundred women. Now, I didn't know how true that was, but he must have been a bad muthafucka if people were going around saying that about him. And if it wasn't true when I first heard it, then it was definitely true by now.

Walking into the student center, I headed straight up to the counseling offices, strolled inside, and headed straight back to Sarah Dexter's office. She'd been my advisor since freshman year, and it wasn't until the end of my junior year that we started fucking. She was only thirty-eight, and the age gap really didn't mean shit to me.

"What's up? Sorry I'm late," I apologized, walking around Sarah's desk and planting a kiss on her cheek as she pushed away from her desk. "I know you miss this dick, and he can't wait to get inside of you."

I took her hand and placed it on top of my erection.

"Why is it that you're always hard when you come into my office?" Sarah asked blankly.

"I don't know. Maybe it's because I'm about to get some pussy."

"Such vulgar language," Sarah replied, undoing my pants. "You're too fine to be talking like that."

Pops said that women were always going to throw up my looks as to why they were having sex with me. I was the spitting image of him, and my mother couldn't stand it. She held a lot of resentment toward him and said that he was the reason why her mother died of a broken heart, but Pops insisted that her mother died because she was a mean old bitch. I wouldn't know one way or the other.

"You're going to have to take it easy today, King. I had to come up with an excuse for my husband because I couldn't have sex for a week," Sarah complained as she stroked my dick. "I had to miss spin class because of the discomfort."

Sarah took my dick inside of her mouth and swirled her tongue around the head.

"Ahhhh… It's not my fault that your husband's dick is too little. Maybe if he was serving you right, you wouldn't have to fuck me to get satisfied."

Sarah deep throated me a few times to drown out my talking. She didn't want to hear anything that came out of my mouth except a moan.

"Oh yeah, Sarah. Your dick sucking abilities are excellent, and I can't wait to get into that pussy."

Sarah spent a few more minutes sucking me off, but Coltrane, also known as my dick, was getting bored because it was taking too long for me to nut. Pulling out of her mouth, I grabbed Sarah up out of the chair and bent her over the desk, raising her little flimsy dress up over her waist.

"Did you remember to lock the door?" Sarah asked nervously. "You forgot the last time, and we almost got caught by Professor Ann."

"She wouldn't have said nothing," came out of my mouth arrogantly. "She would have seen how well I was dusting your pussy off and would have wanted to join in on the action."

Sarah looked back at me and shook her head.

"Shut up and just fuck me, King," she uttered while my hand reached into my pocket and pulled out a gold boy. I tore it open with my teeth and slid the jimmy on tightly.

"Hurry up, King. There's a student coming in forty minutes," Sarah whined.

"This pussy will be dusted off in ten minutes, and if you're a good girl, I'll make you cum back to back."

"That's my favorite when you make me cum back to back," she squeaked. "I sleep like a baby at night when you do that."

Sarah wasn't wet enough for me to enter, so I licked my fingers and got them good and juicy. It was taking too long, and we were on a time restraint, so I plunged them inside of Sarah's aching hole. They went in and out of her until she was ready. Then, I replaced them with the head of my dick, and Sarah almost lost it when she felt the monster entering.

Sarah bit down on her arm and moaned as I pushed in and out of her wetness. Her insides made a farting noise as her walls stretched out, and I worked myself slowly inside of her for a few minutes until her walls opened up fully.

I gripped her hips and replanted my feet then unleashed a relentless assault banging hard deep down inside of her. The swift blows being delivered made her whimper, and she put her hand against my stomach, trying to slow the pace, but my hand knocked it away.

"You're going to take this dick, Sarah Dexter, and I'm going to make you cum in… five… four… three… two… one."

Sarah's walls tightened around my thickness, and her orgasm shot through her like a rocket. She creamed all over me. She moaned uncontrollably as my rod continued pumping inside of her. I wasn't done with her yet, so my hand reached down in between her legs and started rubbing against her clit vigorously. Her muscles tightened around my stiffness once more, and the second orgasm came spilling over shortly after the first one.

"You are so aaaaaammmmmaaazzzziiinnggggg," Sarah moaned as I pushed faster inside of her, and for some reason, Izzy's face popped into my head after hearing the word amazing. A small smile crept onto my face because that's some old head pussy that I was definitely trying to get into soon.

Pulling out of Sarah and releasing all of my content into the condom, I continued to jack it until all of it came out, which was a rule of thumb—Never let the prophylactic fill up inside of a woman because that runs a greater risk of pregnancy.

"Sarah, you are amazing, and I'm glad that we got to spend this time together. Now, pass me those wet wipes."

Sarah reached down and opened up one of her desk drawers, pulling the package out. She placed them on top of some papers, and I grabbed for them joints with the quickness.

"What part of don't pound my pussy like that didn't you under-stand?" Sarah panted.

"I don't know how to do anything else but that," was my response. Pops said never make love to a woman that you don't really care about because if you fuck them all the same, then it's only going to bring problems.

"You liked it… You were moaning and groaning."

"I couldn't help but moan. The way you were aggressively fucking me, I thought you were going to shoot me across my desk," Sarah said, wiping herself off.

"That shit is exciting, isn't it? That's like living on the edge," I joked, throwing my used wet wipes into the trash and pulling up my pants slowly, fastening them. I was ready to go and didn't want to waste any time listening to Sarah whine and complain.

"You know what, Sarah? Since I'm graduating soon, we should call it quits on these little lunch dates. We both know this isn't headed into anything, and you're only using me for sex."

Sarah looked at me and laughed.

"It's funny that you should say that King. I was going to tell you the exact same thing, but in a different way," Sarah confessed. "There have been too many close calls, and my husband has noticed that my vagina has stretched."

"That's fucked up. I didn't mean to stretch you out Sarah, but you feel so good," I said, grabbing her hips and pulling her into me while my hands cupped her breasts and pinched her nipples. You know women like that shit.

Sarah leaned her head back on my shoulder and gasped while being pleasured. Someone came to the door and knocked hard against the glass. It scared the shit out of Sarah, and she jumped away from me.

"That's my appointment! Hurry up and fix yourself," Sarah said startled, tugging at her dress trying to look presentable. "Just one minute!"

"Damn, you look so beautiful when you're flustered," I teased, slapping her ass. Sarah jumped and glared at me with a frown on her face. I threw my hands up in the air and smiled my pearly whites at her.

"You better be lucky that you're gorgeous and have a big dick," Sarah scoffed. "Now, get the hell out of my office, and I'll see you in two weeks."

"I told you that I don't think we should continue this. You're starting to get too attached."

Sarah looked at me and crossed her arms in front of her body defensively.

"I'm your advisor, and you're graduating soon. We need to discuss a few things, and you have to file papers stating that you've completed the required courses for your degree. Don't flatter yourself, King," she said, walking around her desk. "You have a big dick, but you don't know how to use it. You're going to meet a nice young woman, and she's going to whip it on your ass."

I laughed at her because I couldn't believe what she was saying. If I didn't know how to work my dick, she wouldn't be screaming like a banshee and wanting this cold muthafucka up in her.

"Sarah, you're funny. I know how to work my thang, and you've seemed to enjoy it for the past year and half."

Lifting my eyebrow up and walking toward her, I put my hands on her shoulders and kissed the center of her forehead like I always did.

"Besides… a young girl is not going to show me shit, because older women are my preference. Y'all really don't complain about me beating the pussy up, and older women know how to take the D."

Sarah looked me square in the face, frowning.

"Goodbye, Kingdom," Sarah said, pointing at the door.

"I bid you farewell, my lady," I said, bowing to her. I left feeling some type of way because of how Sarah just dismissed me.

LATER THAT NIGHT, I had dinner with my big sister Reece. We tried to get together once a month, but it'd been difficult these past few weeks because she'd been engulfed in one of her court cases. Reece was a tax attorney at a big-time firm, and they were in the middle of an audit. She'd been so busy, and I barely got to see her. I enjoyed our talks because Reece would give me a reality check by keeping me humble, and she was well aware that computers weren't my first choice.

Understanding coding wasn't difficult for me because it came like second nature. My father had me coding at five years old, and I made my first video game at twelve years old. It was never put on the market, but my father was proud of me, and I was proud of myself. That's why my mother pushed me to follow in my father's footsteps.

"What's wrong with you, King? You have that look on your face, and I can't read it," Reece asked, looking concerned.

"Nothing's wrong, sissy," I replied nonchalantly. "I was thinking about life."

Reece gazed at me curiously and smiled then picked up her glass of wine and took a sip.

"So, what did you come up with, little brother?"

"I've found that when you have an overbearing mother it's hard to make life decisions for yourself," I reply sarcastically. "I mean, she talked me into getting a degree in something I have no desire to do. I want to apply for an internship that's in New York. It's an opportunity to work as a photojournalist, and you know taking pictures is my passion."

"That's awesome, King. What type of internship is it?" Reece asked, sitting back in her chair.

"It's an internship for a magazine. Pops says I should go for it and stop being a pussy."

"Sam is right," Reece agreed. "You need to stop being a pussy, and do what makes you happy."

"You guys make it seem like it's so easy," I complained. "Do you know how many times I've heard her say that she'll cut me off if I make a stupid decision that will mess up my life."

"King, your mother doesn't have control over your money. Duchess only has control over what daddy put in the pre-nuptial agreement and what he gives her to spend in the joint accounts. You know he's not going to cut you off."

"Pops says that if she tries to cut me off, he'll make sure that I don't go without," I bragged to Reece, and she smiled at me.

"Pops is going to have you out here slanging dick," Reece said jokingly. "He's a Casanova, and all the ladies love Sam." Reece took a sip of her wine, and it seemed like her thoughts drifted off to somewhere.

"I'm already a dicksmith, and this guy be slanging this cold muthafucka like a six shooter."

"You better be strapping up because STDs are real, my brother," Reece warned. "I know all of these young hoes be throwing you the pussy. Those green eyes and big ass lips make the ladies love King."

"You sound like you're jealous, sis," I teased, setting my fork down on my plate. "Besides, I like older women. Women around your age."

"You like cougar town?" Reece questioned and laughed.

"Let's just say that I like big cat country. I won't discriminate, but I think cougars are a bit too old for me right now. I'll eventually get there, but right now I like panthers."

"So, I'm a... panther?" Reece mocked, laughing even harder. "You young folks come up with more bullshit."

I laughed at my sister because she was always talking about young folks. She was only thirty-five and acted like she was in her fifties sometimes.

"You know you're a panther, Reece, and panthers are sexy in my opinion."

"Don't let your mama hear you talking like that. She'll have you back in therapy in a blink of an eye."

"Please don't remind me of the debauchery. She acted like there was something wrong with me having sex."

"King, you got caught with a woman that was older than your Duchess," Reece reminded me, laughing. "Not to mention, you were seventeen years old."

"Pops was the one who sent her to me, and not everyone's fortunate enough to have a sex tutor to come to their house."

"A sex tutor?" Reece replied blankly. "We're going to change the subject because I'm outdone with that one. Let's settle up the check and go have a drink. I'm over this wine, and I need something a little harder."

"That's cool with me. I need to check my messages, then I'm ready to go."

Reece called the waiter over and grabbed the check. Why couldn't she be my mother? It would make things a lot simpler in my life.

FOUR

Izzy

IT HAD BEEN A LONG DAY, and the night was going to be even longer. I agreed to have dinner at Duchess's house when all I really want to do is crawl up on my couch with a bottle of wine and some Chinese take-out. Jack was specific about what I needed to wear. He said I should go for a more young but sophisticated look to draw the attention of her son, King. I laughed it off because he was being ridiculous, even though King did blow a kiss at me. I wondered what that was about because that young man didn't want my old ass, but he was so damn fine.

Laughing at myself and continuing up the steps, I needed to take a shower and cleanse my face before I started on my mission. There were three looks hanging up in my closet, but I was going to try on at least five more. I was my brand, and the need to slay was prevalent. My face was going to be beat, and my outfit would be stylish. I made a statement no matter what covered my body, and my assets were one thing that always set the mark.

My phone started to ring as soon as I got out of the shower. Making my way over to my vanity to check the screen, of course, it was Jack calling to help me get ready. I hit the icon to answer the FaceTime call.

Jack's face popped up on the screen, and he was already in his regalia. He liked to wear a long black lace front wig with a part straight down the middle and a tiara. He told me that he was from royal blood as well, and we both liked to pretend like we were the queen and princess of LA.

"Hey, sugar. I can't play dress up with you tonight," I said, sitting down in my chair.

"Don't play with me, gurl," Jack scoffed. "You know I called to provide some moral support to you for tonight. You have to look fierce at that dinner because Duchess ain't the only one who's going to be checking you out."

Looking at Jack unamused, my lips turned up in disapproval.

"You're going to have to stop with the insinuating. I told you that I'm not interested in Kingdom."

"He told you to call him King, gurl," Jack replied, rolling his eyes up in his head and fluttering them at me.

"You make me sick, you know that?"

"Ask me if I care?" he replied, pursing his lips. "You know you love me and can't live without my beautiful mug and high cheekbones."

"Bitch, please! I have high cheekbones too," I reminded him. "I think I'm going to be subtle with my makeup, though."

Studying my face in the mirror, my skin was smooth, and the micro-derm abrasion sessions helped to keep the blemishes away.

"Should my brows be natural or done up? Maybe a red lip with just a little mascara?"

"I like where you're going with this, but I need to take a quick sip of my wine to think about it," Jack replied, holding the glass up to his lips and gulping it down.

"Damn, bitch! You were thirsty, huh?" I joked.

"Parched," Jack replied in a snooty tone. "Now, what are you going to wear?"

"I don't know, but whatever it is, it has to make a statement. There are three looks prepared in my closet, but you know I'm going to try on a bunch of other stuff".

"Anything else would be uncivilized," he replied in a snooty tone.

We went on discussing clothing options for tonight while finishing my makeup. I called Jack back on my iPad so that he could help me make some decisions. This process took over an hour, and my driver was due to be at my house in thirty minutes.

DINNER at the McDaniel House

My car service was always prompt, and surprisingly, I was ready when he called to announce that he was out front. I only used the service when going to events or partying in the city because there were two guarantees that would be facing you. The first was that there was never any parking and the second, the price to park was ridiculous. Some lots would charge you up to forty dollars to park your car, and that was how much it was to valet.

We pulled up to Duchess's house, and there was a line of cars parked up and down the street. I noticed people were valeting, and a confused look came across my face because no one mentioned that they were having a straight party.

"You can let me out at the valet stand," I mentioned to Sean. He was my normal driver, and dispatch remembered that I liked for him to come get me. He was a perfect gentleman, and we always had great conversations about everything from fashion to politics. He was able to get me free passes to an exclusive showing of my favorite designer, Gisele, because his girlfriend was a model. I'd been trying to score a booking with her, but it seemed like it was impossible to ever get an appointment.

The valet attendant opened the door and offered me his hand. Grabbing it, I got out of the car looking around at all the people, questioning what I was getting myself into as my feet led me toward the door. There were people checking names, and I hoped that Duchess remembered to add me.

"Can I have your name please?" said the cute girl holding the clipboard.

"Izzy James. Her name was an addition to the list," said a voice from behind me. Turning around to see who said it, Kingdom was facing me, looking handsome.

"I see it right here," the young woman said, smiling. You could tell she was smitten, but I wasn't interested in sticking around to find out.

Bypassing her, I headed into the house, leaving them to converse. All the people standing around the huge atrium took me back, and it was a who's who in black Hollywood. I'd dressed several of them and would love to do business with all of them again as my eyes worked the crowd of people, trying to decide who to go speak to first. It was good manners to go find the hostess of the event since she was the one who invited me, but I felt a bit overdressed in a way.

My look was together, and that's what was important. I decided to wear a pair of black linen harem pants with a white silk tank top, silver sequined stiletto booties, and a short black tuxedo jacket with some long, dangling sequin earrings. The finishing touch were some matching bracelets and a white crystal statement ring enclosed in silver.

"You look cute," said a familiar voice from behind me, making the hairs on the back of my neck stand up, and I knew exactly who it was.

"Kingdom," I said, turning around to face him. "Little girls are cute. I'm a grown woman, and I'm fine, sweetie. Get it together."

I turned my lips up, lifting an eyebrow at him, but it was hard to keep a serious look on my face because he was so damn fine.

"Those facial expressions are so adorable that you keep making. I noticed that at your office and wanted to come kiss those pouty lips of yours," he flirted.

"And you would have gotten slapped too," I replied, putting my hand on my hip. "I'm not a pedophile, and I don't do children."

"That's good because I don't either. I've found that since I've turned twenty-two, my looks have matured some, and I look like I'm eighteen now," King shot back.

We both laughed, and my body managed to relax. It would have been best to stop calling him a child and respect the fact that he was a grown man because he was definitely sexable come to think of it.

"I'm sorry to keep referring to you as a child. I know that you're an adult, but your flirting with me is making me feel uncomfortable," came fumbling out of my mouth, and it was weird.

"Why? Don't men compliment your beauty all of the time? If you were my woman, I would tell you how beautiful you are daily," King said, licking his lips.

"Stop… you're making me blush," I said, fanning myself with my hand. His piercing green eyes were staring a hole right through me, and it was making my lady parts react.

His five-foot-eleven frame was wearing his clothes nicely. You could tell that his muscles had definition by the way his biceps were hugging the tight t-shirt that he had on. I noticed that he was bow legged too. My cousin used to say that bowlegged boys fucked you the best. I'd never experienced it, so I couldn't tell you any different. His package seemed to be lying mid-thigh. He was making women bowlegged by merely having sex with them.

"Can I interest you in something to drink? I know you like wine, and we have several different kinds," King asked pleasantly.

"A glass of wine would be excellent. You can point me in the direction of the bar, and I will get there myself," I replied.

"You don't want me escorting you? Am I cramping your style or something, Miss James?" King asked, narrowing his eyes at me.

"No, not at all," I uttered, frowning. "Why would you ask me something like that?"

"Because you're trying to dismiss me so quickly."

"I'm sorry. I don't mean to be rude or make you feel some type of way," I apologized.

His serious look went back to a smile, and my heart fluttered from his perfectly straight white teeth.

"I wasn't feeling some type of way, but it was fucked up how you were moving," he replied. King held out his arm and looked me up and down. "Now, Izzy, let me escort you over to the bar and get you a drink."

Apprehensively, I wrapped my arm around his and let him lead me over to the bar.

King retrieved me a drink, and we continued to make small talk while I cased the party. Duchess had come into view in a red Zac Posen jumpsuit. I knew it was Zac's design because I had dressed one of my clients in the same one to wear on a talk show.

I could drop names all over the place, but that would be pretentious and so not necessary. I loved fashion, and the women who appreciated a fine garment like the one that was in front of me. Duchess made me think that she was a modern sophisticated lady who knew a lot about designer clothes.

"Don't look now. Here comes my mother," King said, placing his hand on the small of my back. A shiver ran down my spine, and I felt my uterine wall contract. "Ewe, Miss James… I would love to make you shiver like that in a different way."

My eyes darted to him in shock right at the moment Duchess walked up. I couldn't say a word in response to his statement, so I took a sip of wine to gain my composure. This boy didn't know who he was messing with. *Keep playing with fire, and you're going to get burned, Mr. Kingdom McDaniel.*

"Izzy, are you all right?" Duchess asked in concern. "You look a bit flushed."

"Does she?" King questioned, staring at me seductively. "I think she's the perfect shade of caramel."

"King, go find your grandfather," Duchess suggested. "I saw him engaged with a questionable young lady, and I would hope that he has enough sense to pick up on how inappropriate it looks for them to be cozied up on the couch like that."

"Leave Pops alone, Ma," King said, frowning. "He's still a vital old man, and his parts work just as well as mine." King took a drink from his glass, staring directly into my eyes. Turning my head quickly, I took a sip from my glass. That muthafucka was a trip, but I was going to get on that bitch in first class.

"King, can you do what I asked, please?" Duchess insisted.

"Yes, ma'am," King replied dryly, giving me a once over again and smiling. "I'll see you later, Miss James."

"Please, stop calling me, Miss James. Izzy is good enough."

King licked his lips, smiling devilishly at me.

"I bet you play a good naughty school teacher."

"Kingdom!" Duchess said, widening her eyes.

"My fault, Ma. I forgot you were standing right there," King replied. "Later, Izzy."

"Later, King," came out of my mouth with a stupid look on my face.

He walked away, and my eyes followed him lustfully. I wanted to taste his sweet tongue. Not to mention, his breath smelled of peppermints, and it probably tasted minty fresh too.

"Izzy, you'll have to forgive my rude ass son," Duchess said, leaning against the bar. "My father has a big influence over him, and for some reason, King thinks he's a ladies' man."

"Doesn't every man? Can you image walking across a college campus around a bunch of frat boys?" was my reply to the remark, trying to break the tension.

"Oh my God, college was a mess. I had to fight them off with a bat," Duchess uttered, laughing. "My mother, God rest her beautiful soul, said that college was a horny young adult's dream. There were so many men to choose from, and I made sure I got acquainted with a few."

Duchess looked at me coyly, and we both laughed.

"Your house is beautiful. This atrium is giving me life."

"It's one of my favorite places in this house," Duchess replied. "Let me show you the rest of the place because I think you might find inspiration from some of the other rooms."

"That would be great."

Gulping down the last of my wine, I set the glass down on the bar, and Duchess linked arms with me before leading us on our way.

FIVE

King

___

MY MOTHER WAS the biggest cock blocker in the world, bruh! I was working on Izzy, and she walked up and stole my shine. I saw how Izzy was blushing and getting all worked up from my game. If I had a few more minutes with her and another drink, my offer to give her a tour of the house would have been accepted. A tour of the house meant that we would journey upstairs, and that's when I would have went in for the kill.

Duchess was always trying to get me to date the mentees she had running in and out of the house, but I was not interested in none of those chicks, except one. She had a mean head game, and the way she would take my entire dick up her ass, man! Don't get me wrong, I preferred pussy, but playing in the backdoor could be pleasurable too. The freaky chick used to ask me to do it occasionally, and who was I to turn down a request?

"What are you up to, little brother?" my big brother Chester asked, walking up to me.

"Nothing much. Your stepmother is cock blocking again, and I almost embarrassed her by saying something slick to the stylist that's going to be doing her photoshoot for the magazine article."

"Oh yeah. Is she cute?"

"Dogs are cute, bruh. Izzy is a grown woman, and I find her very attractive." Look at me sounding like her.

"Who do you find attractive?" Pops asked, placing his hand on my shoulder.

"Just the man I'm looking for. Where's the young tender that had you hemmed up on the couch?"

He probably had his hand up her dress.

"What you talking about, son?" Pops asked, looking confused. "That wasn't a young tender I was talking too. That girl was busted up and looked like she'd been ran through like the subway in Harlem." We all laughed because Pops was something else. "This old dick would get lost up in that shit."

"That's no good, Pops," was my reaction.

"That's no good, grandson," he agreed.

"You're still the same old Sam, and that's refreshing," Chester said admirably.

"I'm the same ole nigga. Can't get no bigger," Pops stated. "Chess, I know you remember those little trips we used to take a while back."

"I sure do," Chess replied. "I have some of the most fondest memories from going on outings with you."

"A young man is supposed to get his dick wet. Also, you need to test out a variety of different snatch because pussy's not all the same," Sam lectured.

"I thought that wasn't true until I fucked that Asian girl that time we went Vegas," Chess recalled. "Pops got me an Asian prostitute, and that was the smallest pussy that I'd ever fucked. I could only put about a third of my dick inside of her."

"She kept yelling, 'It's too big! It's too big'!" Pops mocked, giving his best impression of the woman. We all laughed because Pops was a lot of fun.

"I thought I was the only person you bought prostitutes for Pops."

"Samuel Crest buys pussy for everyone. I even bought your daddy some pussy the day before he married my daughter, and the two chicks were very accommodating. It was our little secret, and I even tipped them hoes to let him get up in all of their holes," Pops bragged.

"That's why I'm not getting married. I would rather just cohabitate with a woman. That's still having in house pussy," I gave my opinion.

"That's because you haven't met the right woman yet," Chess replied. "I love Athlon, and I haven't cheated on her since we've been married."

"How long has it been?" Pops asked curiously.

"We've been married for six years, but we've been together for ten," Chess replied.

"That's wonderful, but you're going to cheat on her," Pops said, laughing. "It is not in a man's nature to be tied down to one woman."

"Now, I agree with Pops," I spoke up, putting my two cents into the conversation.

"It's just a matter of finding the right one. You'll see, little brother, when you meet the right girl," Chess insisted.

Ma and Izzy were coming down the steps, which meant they just went on a tour of the house. My mama got on my fucking nerves. Her ass needed to go somewhere.

"Why are you looking like that, King?" Pops asked, signaling the bartender.

"Your daughter is the reason." I placed my glass down on the bar, feeling frustrated. "Do you see that woman she's walking with?" Pops and Chess looked around the room until they saw Duchess and Izzy.

"That's Izzy. I know her from college," Chess said nonchalantly.

"Well, that's my future baby mama, and Duchess needs to move out of the way so that I can work my magic. We met her yesterday at her studio, and it was love at first sight." My dick thumped against my leg, and that was a sign for Izzy to be mine.

"She's way older than you, King, and I thought you said you weren't having kids," Chess said, chuckling. I cut my eyes at Chess because he was talking too much.

"And what the fuck does that mean?" Pops asked defensively.

"Exactly," came out of my mouth, and we both stared at Chess smugly. You could tell that he was uncomfortable by the way Chess took a sip of his drink.

"I mean Izzy is around thirty—"

"Three. She's thirty-three years old. I've had sex with women way older than that when I was younger, not to brag or anything."

"How much older?" Chess questioned.

"Let's just say that I've reached cougar status a few times, but Izzy is merely a panther, and I'm on the prowl."

I licked my tongue out and panted like a dog for emphasis because Chess had got me so fucked up.

"That's my boy," Pops cheered. "But if I was your age, I would be knocking down all of these fine young tenderonies."

"I'll take a young thang too. Don't get me wrong, but they don't know what they're doing. A lot of them are inexperienced and don't know how to perform oral sex."

"That's why you have to teach them, King. Have you been paying any attention to the game that I've been giving to you over the years?" Pops questioned.

"Yeah Pops, but I like a seasoned woman. A woman who knows how to tighten that grip around my dick while she's throwing it back and making that ass clap."

Chess looked at me strangely then shook his head in disbelief.

"Not only do you look like this man, but you sound just like him too," Chess proclaimed.

"What are you guys up to over here doing?" Chester Senior asked, walking up.

"We're just watching asses and camel toes," Pops replied happily.

"It's a lot of it flowing through here," Chester Senior pointed out. "There's a girl walking around here in a swimsuit and a sarong. I thought we were having a pool party at first, but she informed me that she had just left the beach. I guess our conversation was going on too long because Duchess came over and broke it up."

"Her conscience must have been eating at her," Chess mumbled. Dad looked behind him at Chess and held up his glass.

"Touché' son, but your mother was a real bitch," Dad shot back.

"She says the same thing about you," Chess replied, putting down his glass on the bar and walking off before dad could respond.

"I think he still hasn't gotten over the fact that me and his mother fell out of love," my dad said solemnly.

"You ain't fall out of love with his mother. My daughter was younger, and she fucked you better," Pops said frankly. "That doesn't make you a bad guy, Chester. It just makes you an asshole."

IT'D BEEN over an hour since an Izzy sighting, and I couldn't find her anywhere. It was almost like she disappeared, but Chelsea said that she hadn't left the party. Maybe sitting in one place would help me spot her walking around. My eyes drifted to Pops over on the couch, and it looked like he was watching ass, so I decided to go join him. He was in a neutral spot, and my field of vision was in good view of everyone's coming and goings. I'd been trying to duck my mother because she had that look on her face when she spotted me thirty minutes ago. I was sure she wanted to bitch me out about the comments I made to Izzy, but I did think she'd play the sex teacher role really well, and if I had the chance to live that fantasy out, I'd be forever grateful to Izzy James, the naughty school teacher.

Making my way over to the couch to sit down next to my Pops, the vibe of the party was pretty cool. He was engaged in a conversation with some random chick, and she damn near lost her mind when she saw me. She kept commenting on how much Pops and I looked alike, and he almost convinced her into a threesome with the both of us. My interest wasn't there, but Pops seemed very excited, so I excused myself and went to the bathroom to hide out from my freaky grandfather and his sexual capers.

Coming out of my room, I stopped at the top of the steps, looking out into the sea of people. I was feeling defeated because I couldn't find Izzy, but then she appeared over by bar. It looked like she was talking to some guy, and a girl was lingering near them. Izzy looked very uncomfortable, and it appeared that the dude was getting a kick out of it. The woman standing near them had a smug smile on her face, but her body language displayed something different. I noticed that she stayed behind the man, even when she said something to Izzy. It was almost like Izzy was punking her, and the guy was being her protector.

I continued to watch them, waiting for the opportunity to go talk with Izzy. She looked so beautiful mad, and I would have loved to help her work off all of that aggression. I'd beat that juice box up with ten inches of hard dick and make her cum all over it.

The thoughts must have made me drift off because when I came back to reality, Izzy picked up her drink and spilled it all over old boy. She stormed off from the scene and got lost in the crowd. It was difficult to keep my eyes planted on her, but as soon as she made it halfway in, I didn't see her anymore.

What was all of that about because Izzy was pissed off! I wondered if she used to mess with the guy, and the girl was the new boo.

The need to find Izzy to make sure that she was okay was a must. I'd be the hero in this situation and that damsel in distress could repay me with the golden ticket in between her legs. It's a win win situation for both of us.

SIX

Izzy

OUT OF ALL THE dinner parties in LA, why did Craig and Yoshi have to be at this one? I spotted them when I was walking around the party with Duchess. Yoshi's giraffe neck ass was the first person I saw, and Craig wasn't too far away.

A part of me felt a little bad because I had Duchess pegged all wrong. She was uptight and pretentious, but she was not a snob like I thought she would be. We had a very interesting conversation about her views on politics and religion. It was a no brainer that she was a Baptist, but I was surprised to hear that she dabbled in a little Scientology when she was younger. Duchess claimed that she was very adventurous when she was younger, but once she met Chester Senior, it changed her entire outlook on life.

After the tour, my hiding space consisted of a large tree that sat in the corner by some long glass windows. You wouldn't be able to spot me unless you were actually near there, and for some reason, it felt safe. Craig and Yoshi weren't the only people that I didn't want to run into. That Kingdom made me horny by looking at him, and I really wanted to fuck that young man. His arrogant demeanor and those sexy ass eyes made a bitch want to swing low. The print of his thang in those damn skinny jeans was life. Come to think of it, that was the only good use for a man to wear those pants. I bet his nuts hurt from the way they were clinging to his body. They gave a new meaning to "my nuts are heavy" because those bad boys were all jumbled up inside of that tiny little space.

I laughed at myself because all of those glasses of wine were catching up to me. The best course of action would be to find the food spread to eat and soak up some of the alcohol I consumed. Duchess said there was every type of meat a person could want to eat, and there was a fresh fruit and veggies tray that had my name all over it.

The bar wasn't that far, so I grabbed my glass and made my way to the kitchen without being spotted. It was key to case the room before I made my move. I maneuvered through the crowd easily, but as soon as I made it halfway to the door, someone called out my name.

"Elizabeth James!"

Shit... someone noticed me, came to mind as my head dropped down. I heard my name again, and my shoulders hunched as I slowly turned around to see who was calling me.

"Oh my God! Athlon McDaniel! How the hell are you, soror?"

"I'm blacktastic," Athlon replied. We did our secret sorority handshake and hugged one another.

"It's so good to see you, Gamma Girl."

"It's good to see you too," Athlon replied.

I took in how beautiful she looked in her bright orange swing dress that blended absolutely fantastic against her dark ebony skin.

"I love this color on you. You know I've always been jealous of your dark skin."

"I remember," Athlon replied and laughed. "I feel like a circus tent in this dress, though. I'm six months pregnant and starting to show."

"Show where? The only things I see standing out are those large knockers on your chest." My face drew up into a frown, and we both laughed, hugging one another again. "I was about to go get some food. Would you like to join me?"

"Sure," Athlon replied. "I'm always hungry, so the mention of food will always cause me to follow you."

It made me happy to see Athlon after all of these years. The last time we were together was about three years ago when I helped her with the launch of her very first jewelry collection, then we lost touch after that.

"I see that you're doing big things, Athlon. I saw the editorial that they did on you in Essence, and I ordered a few pieces to add to my accessory closet."

"No… you're the one doing big things, Izzy. I heard that you helped style two shows during fashion week this year. I had a designer reach out to me and got a few pieces put in their show," Athlon mentioned.

"You know I could talk to a few of my celebrity clients and have them rock some of your jewelry. As a matter of fact, I would like to use a few of your pieces for Duchess's photoshoot." Athlon looked at me and cut her eyes.

"I'll pass," Athlon uttered and looked around the room. "That woman is ridiculous, and I'd rather put my jewelry on a circus monkey and have him run around the ring playing with his ass before I let that woman represent my jewelry line."

"Damn, that's harsh," I said, feeling a bit uncomfortable. Athlon must have picked up on it because she put her hand on my shoulder and laughed.

"I'm sorry Izzy," she apologized. "It's just me and that woman do not get along. I think she's pretentious, arrogant, tacky, and a fraud. She tries to make herself appear to be innocent in a high and mighty way, but how can you be that way when you stole your husband from his first wife?"

"I remember when Chester Senior was going through the divorce. It was a lot on Chess when he found out that his father had been having an affair and that he had a six-year old brother. We spent a lot of nights up drinking, not that we really needed an excuse to do it."

"Well, the relationship between Chess, Reece, and Duchess is pretty much nonexistent. We spend a lot of time with King, but he's not a big fan of his mother either. She tries to control that poor boy's life, and all he wants to do is live it on his own terms."

"He's an aggressive young man," I said slightly frowning. "Do you know he was flirting with me? I'm old enough to be his mother, but that doesn't seem to deter him. It seems like it's driving him further to want to get in my pants."

Athlon laughed as we made our way into the kitchen. My stomach started to growl, and it was time to smash some of the food. Everything looked so delicious.

"King is a bit of a lady's man. They seem to fall all over him, but have you met his grandfather Samuel?" Athlon asked. "He'll be all over you too if he saw your beautiful ass."

We both laughed strolling over to the sink. I washed my hands while Athlon filled me in on all of the history of her in-laws. I knew who Duchess's father was from a long time ago. It wasn't that long ago, but it seemed like it when I began to think back to my mid-twenties.

"Speaking of the devil, there he goes right there," Athlon said, pointing at Sam. That was definitely Ash's Smokey Robinson impersonator. Ash said her mother had a crush on the actual singer when she was growing up.

"He still looks good to be an old man," I said before taking a bite of my chicken. "It's like he's a vampire and will never age."

King came up behind Sam and said something to him. It looked like he was annoyed, but I was not trying to find out what was going on with him.

THE MEAL WAS AWESOME, and it was time for me to get another drink. Catching up with Athlon was fun, and we made plans to collaborate on a few projects. She even agreed to let me get a few pieces to use for Duchess's photoshoot. Reminding her that it was more about the exposure than it was the person brought it home for me. It was important to be able to work a person without them knowing it.

I made my way up to the bar, ready to get a big ass glass of excellence. I went to the bathroom and checked my blood sugar, which was low enough for me to have at least three more glasses of wine. It was really one... but you know how that goes.

Signaling the bartender, he smiled because he must have remembered me from earlier. I kind of embarrassed myself by grabbing the bottle of wine and refilling my glass, but he was busy, and I refilled two other people's glasses around me. That was doing him a solid, wouldn't you think?

"I didn't know you knew Duchess."

My body cringed when I heard Craig's voice because I'd done so well in avoiding him.

"Excuse me! I'm going to need two glasses," I called to the bartender before turning around to find Craig standing behind me with Yoshi standing off to the side of him. "I've been working so hard to avoid you tonight, Craig. If I close my eyes real tight, will you disappear when I open them?"

I closed my eyes mentally counting to ten, hoping like hell he'd go away. Opening them slowly, Craig was still standing in front of me, but damn his ass was fine as hell. There was a striking resemblance between Craig and King. They both were redbones with those got damn eyes. Craig was taller than King and had a little bit more weight over him, so evidently, this girl must have a thing for light skinned men with green eyes. Which led me to believe they were going to be the death of me.

"C'mon, Craig. I want to go grab a piece of fruit or something from the buffet," Yoshi whined in an annoying voice.

"Wait a minute, baby," Craig said, putting up his hand. "I'm trying to have a conversation with Izzy."

"You haven't taught your child manners yet? Maybe if you go get her some fruit, she'll sit like a good girl and let you talk to mama."

It was a cheap shot, but fuck him and her.

"I'm not going to stand here and listen to her insult me, Craig," Yoshi demanded then stomped her foot.

"Ohhhh... Yoshi is mad, Craig, and about to throw a tantrum."

I could tell the both of them were aggravated, but so what? He should have kept on going and left me the fuck alone.

"Grow up, Izzy. Yoshi acts way more mature than how you're behaving right now. I don't know what you have against her, but I'm really starting to see how jealous you are of her," said Craig, smiling smugly, and that totally pissed me off.

"You wish I was jealous of this anorexic ass bitch, but that's what you want me to be... jealous of her, and that's why you try to throw her up in my face. However, I could care less about either of you muthafuckas. How about that!"

The people around us stared for a second, but neither one of us cared who heard what I said because it was between the both of us.

"Oh... you care, Izzy. That's why you're trying to make a big scene in front of all of these people." Craig hissed.

"Oh... I'll make a scene for your ass."

I picked up one of the glasses of wine, pouring it on Craig's shirt while Yoshi watched, laughing. Next, I swooped the other glass up off the bar, storming toward Yoshi. She threw her hands up in front of her face trying to shield it from me.

"Please, don't throw that on me!" Yoshi begged.

I looked at her while laughing hysterically.

"Guuuurrrrlllll... I'm not about to waste any more of this good ass wine. This here will be drank by me," I relayed, rolling my eyes as I kept it moving past her, but I made sure my shoulder bumped her ass hard.

There was a group of girls standing over by the bar when I made my exit, and one of them gave me a high five. I was pissed off to the highest point of pissocity, but I had to calm it down because it was someone else's house.

Chugging down my drink, I made my way over to the bar on the patio. People were all around partying and having a good time. But my black ass was agitated, and a drink would make a bitch feel a little better.

"Garcon! Can I please have a scotch on the rocks with a dash of soda," I called out. He must have seen the stress on my face because he fixed that drink rather quickly. Placing it down in front of me, I swallowed it down fast.

"Let me get another one!" I yelled out.

He looked at me and smiled before walking away to get me another drink. Opening up my purse, I noticed the joint for emergency purposes sitting on my compact, looking ever so lovely. I had a feeling that some shit was going to pop off, so I put the little beauty in my clutch.

The bartender placed the drink in front of me, and a warm smile spread across my lips. Reaching into my purse, I pulled a ten-dollar bill out, handing it to him.

"Thank you for being so prompt."

"What's in that glass?" King said, pressing his body against mine. Reaching around my waist and taking my drink out of my hand, he took a sip.

"Damn, that's strong."

"Give me back my drink, lightweight," I said, taking my drink back and knocking it down. I put the glass on the bar, pushing my ass against his dick. "Now, if you'll excuse me, I need to take a smoke break."

Turning around to face him, I licked my lips seductively. A slight smile played on his lips, making me want to kiss those juicy muthafuckas.

"Can you move please so I can go smoke my joint?"

"You have a joint? Can I hit it?" King asked seductively. I smiled at him, leaning in close.

"I've got something else you can hit, and it's much better than this joint." I stepped to the side and headed for the hills because I was about to stir up some trouble.

THERE WAS a secluded area in the near distance, and it looked like some place where I could go to be alone to smoke my joint in peace. There was a bush sitting next to a bench, so I decided to settle myself there. I hoped Kingdom didn't see me pour my drink on Craig, but in all actuality, I really didn't give a shit because Craig deserved what he got.

SEVEN

Craig

THE PATIO WAS LIVE, and the music was pumping. I stepped out the doors shortly after the little scene with Izzy, and the first thing I saw was some young nigga all up in Izzy's face. He was standing a little too close for comfort, and if they kissed, I was definitely going to make a beeline over there. Izzy would not disrespect me twice in one night because her ass still belonged to me. So what that I was there with another woman? I knew it was selfish, but truth be told, I needed Izzy in my life. She kept me grounded and humbled in a good way, even though I wanted to harm her sometimes. She had a smart-ass mouth and a really bad temper. I was surprised she even had people working for her because the way she cussed at her staff, it was a wonder they hadn't all quit.

I watched as Izzy blew past ole boy, and he turned to watch her walk away. I noticed that dude kind of looked like me, but he was young and should've been in bed. There was no way he was over eighteen.

I decided to go strike up a conversation with him because I was curious to know what was going on between the two of them. This lil' dude needed to know that Izzy was way too mature for him, and her ass was already spoken for.

"This is one dope party," I casually mentioned to the youngster, and he looked me up and down before responding.

"My mother always throws a good party," he replied dryly.

"Duchess is your mother? I've heard her talk about you, but this is the first time I've seen you. I'm Craig Madison from Stardust Production Agency."

He turned, continuing to look for a moment, checking me out. I knew I was a handsome muthafucka, but I didn't play with punks.

"Aren't you the dude that Izzy threw the drink on?" he asked smugly. "Did you come over here to see who I was since you saw us talking?" This little bastard had me fucked up by talking shit to me.

"Izzy spilled her drink on me by accident." I tried to play it off.

"It looked like she poured that bad boy on you, and I must say that you handled it like a champ, especially how you tied the shirt around your waist. I guess you picked up some fashion tips from Izzy. Did the two of you mess around?"

"Why do you figure we messed around?" My curiosity was piqued. He took a sip of his drink and raised his eyebrows.

"Well, a woman only throws her drink on a man who's harassing her, being an asshole, or is an ex-boyfriend," he explained. "I saw you with that tall chick, so I assumed that you and Izzy got into it about her." I signaled the bartender to get a drink. Who did this snot nosed kid think he was anyway?

"I'm not Izzy's ex. Matter of fact, I'm her current, and we're just having a few issues right now."

"So you're Izzy's man? She didn't mention having a boyfriend. I guess I had the situation wrong. I'll have to speak to her about that small detail."

"Are the two of you talking or something?" came out of my mouth without hesitation. She had better not be letting another nigga smash, especially not that little dude. He looked like he could be our son. "If you don't mind me asking… how old are you?"

Dude stared at me strangely then smirked.

"Izzy and I just became acquainted yesterday. I found her strikingly beautiful, and I wanted to get to know her better," he replied. "Far as how old I am…" He looked at me arrogantly with the utmost confidence. "I'm old enough to knock Izzy down and make her beg for more of this big dick." He finished off his drink and sat the glass on the bar. "Now if you'll excuse me, I need to go find out where my future baby mama is so that I can rub on her booty. You really pissed her off, and I would really hate it if you've ruined her night. The plan was to take her back to my house and knock her back out. It's obvious you're not doing your job, and now I can see why she's so uptight." He patted me on my shoulder then walked off nonchalantly.

"Little boy, I'll…" and before I could get the words out of my mouth, he had disappeared into the crowd.

That pissed me off, and a drink was desperately needed. I called the bartender again, and he finally made his way down to me. I ordered a shot of cognac straight and took it straight to the head as soon as he put it in front of me. Scanning the crowd for Izzy was impossible, but I had a bone to pick with her because she wasn't going to beat me at my own game with a mini me.

EIGHT

Izzy

"CAN AN OLD FRIEND JOIN YOU?" asked Samuel Crest, standing in front of me.

"Wow… How the hell are you, Sam?" I asked, scooting over to make room for him. "You're still looking fine as ever."

"Why thank you, baby," Sam replied and sat down. "You're still a beauty as well."

"Why thank you, Sam," rolled off my tongue, and a giggle came out because years of memories came flooding back to me. "You still smoke weed?"

He took it from me without any convincing. He hit it two times and held on to the smoke for a few seconds before he blew it out.

"This is the exact reason why I came out here," Sam confessed. "I didn't want to be too close to the house because my daughter would be bitching and complaining." He handed me the joint back and smiled. "She has a room designated for smoking, but my grandson is around here somewhere, and I can't seem to find him to go with me."

"That boy needs to keep his distance from me because I'm getting tired of fighting his ass up off of me. He keeps rubbing his dick against my ass, and I'm trying to be a lady about the situation."

Sam looked over at me and laughed.

"Yeah... that boy has a lot of his grandfather in him, and I'm proud of it. He recognized a thoroughbred and... he needs a few thick thangs in his stable."

I looked at Sam appalled because he just compared me to a horse.

"Why are you looking at me like that, Izzy? You know I'm a muthafucka when it comes to the ladies, and we shared a few good times together, wouldn't you say?"

My hand went over my mouth because he had me there, and it was refreshing to see that he was still the same dirty old man.

"I bet you'd probably encourage Kingdom to pursue me, wouldn't you?" I asked curiously.

"Damn right!" he replied shamelessly. "I encourage King to explore his sexual appetite and never limit himself to the standards of others. Now, I don't condone him fucking boys, but if that's what he decided to do, I would still love him all the same."

"I don't think he's gay, Sam." Lord, at least I hoped not.

"I know he's not gay, but I'm just saying, Izzy. I'm supportive of my grandson in everything that he does. I'm even more proud of him because he'll be graduating from college in the spring, and he can finally get away from my worrisome ass daughter."

I looked at him and giggled because it was surprising to hear him say that, but Sam used to always complain about how extra his daughter was when we used to hang with him.

"Can I ask you a question?"

He lifted his eyebrows at me smiling.

"Shoot," Sam replied while I hit my joint one last time and put the roach out on the bench. I turned to face him for the answer to this question.

"Have you talked to Ash? We lost touch, and I miss her so much."

Sam smiled at me and looked around for a second before he answered the question.

"I talk to Ash everyday," Sam replied. "We have a nine-year-old son together, and I go visit them at least twice a week. She lives in

Long Beach and moved there when we found out that she was pregnant."

"Damn! I had no idea," I uttered in disbelief. "I remember telling her ass that she was pregnant, but she didn't believe me."

"She was in fact pregnant, and I had to beg her not to get rid of it," Sam added solemnly. "Ash is like my safe haven, and I had to move her closer to me so that I could have a relationship with my child."

"Do you mind me asking what's his name? I would really like to talk to Ash."

"His name is Samuel, after me, and I'm sure she would love to speak with you," Sam replied. "However, you must never speak of this to Duchess. She doesn't know about Sam, and I want to keep it that way."

A surprised expression came across my face, but I wasn't going to betray his trust. We went back a long way, and it was not my business to tell.

Sam and I sat and continued to talk for a while. He fired up his joint, and we laughed at the memories that we shared together. We must have looked like we were having a good time because Duchess walked up on us, and she didn't look too enthused.

"I see the two of you are over here getting cozy," Duchess spat. "Izzy is my daddy over here trying to get you to thot yourself out to him? A lot of women are thirsty in this day and age. They see a wealthy man and assume that he'll trick his money off."

I glared up at her with "bitch, please" written all over my face. This was the third person who had me fucked up tonight, and I was going to have to put her ass in her place.

"Duchess, you're being rude as hell, and it's embarrassing," Sam fussed. "I've known Izzy for well over ten years, and we were just catching up on old times."

"And for the record, I've never fucked your father, nor do I intend on fucking him. You should never assume anything because you just made an ass out of you and not me." Getting up off the bench, I straightened my clothes. "Now, if you both would excuse me. I really have to use the bathroom." I kissed Sam on top of his forehead, smiling at him warmly. "I'll be looking forward to having lunch with you soon, Sam." Pulling my business card out of my clutch, I handed it to him then sashayed off to go pee, doing my best walk. I doubled back because I had something to ask Sam, but instead I overheard an uncomfortable exchange between him and Duchess that made me cringe.

"You were way out of line, Duchess," Sam hissed. "I'm sure you embarrassed Izzy, and she might not want to work with you now that you called her a thirsty thot."

"I did not call her that," Duchess scoffed, looking behind her. "I just know your angle and wanted to come assess the situation so that you wouldn't mess up my photoshoot. I was afraid that you were over here hitting on her, and I couldn't let that happen."

Sam looked at his daughter in disgust.

"Why is that Duchess? I can't help it if young women find me irresistible."

"They find your money irresistible, daddy," Duchess hissed. "You're damn near seventy, and you're still trying to throw that old shriveled up dick around like it's the crown jewel or something. Maybe if you would have learned how to keep that thing in your pants, my mother wouldn't have died of a broken heart!" Sam looked at Duchess with contempt in his eyes, but he couldn't argue with her because Gloria did die of a broken heart.

"I can't change that Duchess, and I've apologized to you a million times for it," Sam replied. "I am human, and we all make mistakes. When are you going to forgive me for it?"

"Never!" Duchess hissed, storming off. Sam shook his head pulling out a cigarette. He couldn't make Duchess forgive him, and he wasn't going to keep trying either.

I MANAGED to make it to the bathroom and didn't realize how drunk I actually was until sitting down on the toilet. I couldn't believe that bitch came for me as if I wanted Sam. The gag would have been me telling her that her damn son was a thirsty thot trying to get into my panties. I wondered how she would react to that. Duchess had me feeling some type of way, and I should go back out there and curse her ass out.

I got up off the toilet without pee running down my leg. Sometimes when you're drunk, you don't wipe that well and mishaps happen. People pass judgment, but we're all guilty of it. I wondered how many men had pee stains in the front of their underwear because they didn't thoroughly shake their dick. A person should never have no problems accepting shortcomings because a drunk ain't shit, and all kinds of randomness happens when you're leveled.

My hands were clean and dry before leaving out of the bathroom. I put some of the hand lotion they had sitting on the sink in my palm, rubbing them together. Before leaving out, I prayed that I didn't run into anyone that pissed me off. There were about three people at the party that were on my shit list, and I would hate to have to go upside somebody's head over some bullshit.

Slowly opening the door, I took a few steps out, looking around to see if the coast was clear. There wasn't a hater in sight as I went walking down the hallway until I made it to the top of the staircase. My brain was trying to figure out exactly where to go, so I reached down into my pocket, grabbing my phone. It was pretty late and time for me to go home since my head was drunk, my body horny, and all of me was in need of some sleep. If that wasn't a deadly combination, then I didn't know what was.

"There you go! Where have you been, beautiful?" King said, wrapping his arms around my waist and kissing my neck softly.

"You're going to stop playing with me, little boy. You keep pressing your dick against me, and I'm going to end up showing you something." King laughed heartily, squeezing me tightly.

"Does this feel like a little boy to you?" he asked, leaning me forward slightly and pressing his thickness against my butt.

"Hell naw, that ain't little! Let me see it because I want to know if that anaconda is actually real."

I spun around, smiling at him but almost lost my balance. He held me up while I giggled uncontrollably because I was too fucked up to be embarrassed by my actions. And if his punk ass wanted to be aggressive, then I was about to take him down that way.

"You want some of this grown lady pussy don't, you, son? Don't you know I'll turn your ass out and send you crying home to your mother?"

King stood there smiling at me with a glimmer in his eyes, and it seemed like he was amused by my words. It felt like he wasn't taking me serious, so I took it upon myself to show his ass something by pushing him backward into the wall. Somehow, we got tangled up in the large curtains, and it hid us away from the rest of the party.

My hand journeyed down and cupped his dick. I moved it up and down because I wanted to know how it felt hard. My lips kissed his neck, placing my mouth next to his ear, moaning softly into it. King's breathing became shallow and stagnant. I could tell that he was turned on by the way he pulled me closer and his hands gripped my ass. I must have really worked myself up too because the next thing I knew, my tongue was pushing inside of his mouth.

We were kissing nastily as my hand continued to stroke his dick. He was hard as a muthafucka, and I wanted to put it in my mouth. I broke away from King, and he took over from there. I felt soft wet kisses on my neck, and my nipples strained against the fabric of my bra.

"I want you," King whispered in my ear.

"I want you too," I said breathlessly. "I want to make you cum."

"I want you to make me cum too," he groaned. His rod stiffened in my hand even more as he gripped my ass much tighter. "I want to taste that sweet pussy."

"I just bet you do," I mocked. "You want to put this monster inside of my sopping wet pussy too… don't you?"

"Yes." He sighed heavily. "I want to tear that shit up."

He kissed my lips firmly, and I received his tongue without protest. I was still working him in my hand, and it felt like he was about to release when I heard Duchess call his name. It was like she snapped me out of a trance, and my ass sobered up real quick. I released his package from my hand and stepped back. King stared at me clueless as I started walking backward out of the curtain.

"Your mama's looking for you. She's calling your name."

Duchess called his name again, and I turned in the direction it was coming from because I was about to go in the other direction. She was the last person I wanted to see us together because a good cussing was guaranteed with that one.

"Izzy, wait!" King called out, coming from behind the curtain. I walked back over to him and smiled wickedly.

"Our fun has ended, King, and it's a shame you didn't bust."

Kissing his lips quickly, I slipped away and didn't look back.

NINE

King

I STARED in disbelief as I watched Izzy's go down the steps. She looked amused that my mother came, but I couldn't understand why. I was about to nut when that woman started calling my damn name, and that's why Izzy stopped her voodoo. I had never had a woman stroke my dick like that, and she was doing it through my jeans.

"There you are, King," Duchess said, walking up. "Where did you just come from?"

I glared at her for a second because I was really pissed off.

"I just came out of the curtain. What do you want?" I replied dryly. Noticing I had a bit of an attitude, her eyebrow lifted at me.

"I was looking for you because Chelsea wanted to hang out," my mother explained.

"Why does she want to hang out with me? She's your assistant, so wouldn't it be best if the two of you hung out? I don't need a babysitter anymore, Ma. I'm a grown man. You seem to keep forgetting that," I said, seething. "Me and that girl don't have nothing in common, and I told you that I'm not interested in her. How many times do I have to tell you that?"

"Excuse me, grumpy, but I didn't just piss in your Cornflakes."

Duchess hissed. "All I was doing was delivering a message. You don't have to talk to me like that, King."

I stared at her for a second because I almost told her that she interrupted one of the best experiences of my life. She better hope that I didn't get blue balls, or else I was going to walk through the entire house smoking the loudest weed I could find.

"I don't know what's wrong with the men of this family tonight. I had to go there with your grandfather because it looked like he and Izzy were getting real close and personal in the backyard."

"When was this?" I asked nosily. I knew Pops was not trying to push up on Izzy because if he was, there was going to be a problem.

THE NEXT DAY

I agreed to meet Pops at Roscoe's Chicken and Waffles in Hollywood. This was one of his favorite places to eat because it held so many memories for him. I parked my black on black, four door Porsche in the parking lot and headed toward the door. Spotting my grandfather's car as I approached the line, I figured he'd already had a booth, and I maneuvered on into the restaurant.

"Over here, King!" Pops yelled.

Looking over to my left, he was at the usual corner booth that he liked to sit in. I made my way over to him with a few questions that I needed to ask him. I couldn't get out of my head that my mama said Izzy and Pops were being cozy in the yard. I wanted to know if he was trying to get on her because if that was the case, he needed to stand down. That pussy was mine.

"Hey, Pops, what's up?" I said, giving him some dap.

"Nothing much, King. Did you make it to class this morning? It was a late night for all of us," Pops replied, smiling. "I took this cute little number over to one of my houses last night and ran her down real quick. I noticed you were missing in action, so I assumed you left with someone?" Staring at him for a second, I hoped he wasn't talking about Izzy.

"Pops, did you fuck Izzy last night?" I just came out and said it.

"What are you talking about, King?" he questioned, laughing. "Did your mother tell you some nonsense about Izzy and I?"

"She said the two of you were very cozy in the yard last night," I explained. "You know I'm trying to get on her, don't you?"

A big smile spread across my grandfather's face. He studied me closely before he decided to speak.

"Calm down, youngster," he said. "I've know Izzy for a very long time, and we have a history together."

I dropped my head and grabbed my temples. There was no way I could fuck with her now if she used to fuck with Pops.

"It's not what you think, King. We never slept together. I take that back. There was this one time that we were in Vegas, and we got so high and drunk that some shit popped off. I didn't actually penetrate her, but I did taste that sweet pussy."

Staring at my Pops, I had a blank expression on my face.

"That's all bad, Pops," I said, groaning. "I wanted to get all up in those guts because I find her so sexy."

"You can still get up in those guts, son. I used to mess with a good friend of Izzy's. We were never involved with each other. We're just friends," he explained, eating his food.

"I don't know, Pops. I don't want her hashing out some old feelings that she has for you. "

"That's something you don't have to worry about, King. We were never interested in each other like that, and like I said, we were just friends," Pops assured me.

"Good." I sighed. "Because we got real close and personal last night in the curtains."

Pops looked at me strangely.

"In the curtains?" he questioned, lifting an eyebrow. I looked at him and smiled while the waiter put our food on the table. Pops knew what I liked to eat, so he took the liberty of ordering my food before I arrived. The waiter made sure that we were straight, and I waited until he left before I told Pops what happened.

"I caught Izzy coming from the bathroom and walked up behind her, wrapping my arms around her waist. I kissed her on the neck like you taught me, and I could feel her melting in my arms."

"Go on," said Pops enthusiastically, pouring syrup on his waffles.

"I pressed my dick against her ass, and before I knew it, she was pushing me into the curtains. I wasn't sure what she had in mind, but I was going to be a willing participant either way."

"My boy!" Pops gloated and gave me a five. "I taught you well son, and I hope you capitalized on the situation."

"Maaannnn… did I!" I said excitedly.

I looked around and saw a few people staring at me, so I sat back in the booth for a second to calm down. I couldn't sleep at all last night and had to beat my meat twice in order to get my erection to calm the fuck down.

"Pops, I have never experienced being jacked off with my pants on," I said, bragging. "She was gripping my joint, stroking it real good while she was kissing me nastily all in my mouth."

"Ah, King. You let her kiss you?" Pops asked, frowning. "What is the number one rule to the game?"

"Never kiss a woman because it's too intimate," I replied dryly. "I know what the rule is, Pops, but I welcomed her kisses gladly. Her tongue tasted sweet, and she's a really good kisser."

"How do you know that she's a really good kisser? How many women have you kissed?"

I stared at my grandfather in disbelief because he was sounding like a hater.

"I've kissed a few broads before Pops. I told you that my nanny Francine taught me how to kiss."

"I remember old Francine. I used to dust her off occasionally when I would come over to your house to visit," Pops bragged arrogantly.

"I was too young to know what she was doing, but every time I saw her, I would make sure that I got a kiss," I remembered. "Anyway… let me finish telling you."

Pops put a piece of chicken in his mouth and chewed it.

"Eat your food, King, before it gets cold," he suggested.

"Man, Pops… fuck this food. I think I've found the perfect woman for me, and all you're worried about is my food getting cold?" I questioned.

A smile came across Pops face, and he sat his fork down to give me his undivided attention.

"Pops, my dick was so hard that it was throbbing. We were whispering shit into each other's ear, and it was turning me on."

"Did you close the deal?" Pops asked curiously.

I looked at him with a disgusted look on my face.

"Nope. Right when I was about to bust my nut, Duchess called out my name and messed up everything. It was like we were in the coatroom at school sneaking around. Ma completely messed everything up, and Izzy teased me about it," I explained. I picked up one of my chicken wings and broke it open.

"I was so pissed at my mama that I wanted to curse her ass out."

Pops laughed at me, and I didn't see any humor in the shit at all.

"Why are you laughing?"

"Because the look on your face, King, is priceless. Did you get blue balls, son?" Pops joked.

I stared at him unamused as I ate my food.

"I don't find it funny, Pops. This woman had me gone, and all she was doing was jacking me off through my jeans."

"Let me tell you something about a woman like Izzy. She's been trained, and she knows what she's doing," Pops replied frankly.

"What do you mean 'she's been trained?'" I asked curiously. "She used to be a prostitute?"

"Not exactly," Pops replied. "Izzy used to work for a premier escort service. She wasn't serving the Johns, but she had several friends that were in the business. I remember paying for her and this girl named Ash to take a class on Karma Sutra."

"Isn't that the Indian book that teaches you how to fuck?" I asked inquisitively. "Maybe I need to pick that bad boy up."

Pops laughed, wiping his mouth with his napkin.

"You're close, King. It's a Sanskrit guide to sexual technique, sexual behavior, and love. It tells you how to have sex and gives you positions in order to achieve an orgasm," he replied.

"How do you know so much about it?" I questioned, looking at him accusingly.

"Funny you should ask, grandson. Ash used some of the moves

she learned on me. However, I used to mess around with a Kama Sutra expert."

"Of course, you did," I uttered, laughing. "Well, I'm going to pursue Miss Elizabeth James, and she's going to give this brother some of that good stuff."

"How do you know it's good?" Pops questioned, putting a piece of waffle in his mouth. "Yeah, she looks good on the outside, but how do you know that she has some good pussy?"

"I can just tell by the way she walks," I replied, chuckling. "Also, I met this dude that fucks with Izzy, and he was all up in my grill, trying to question me about her."

"A boyfriend maybe?"

"I don't think he's her boyfriend. He mentioned something about them messing around, but I saw Izzy dump her glass of wine on him at the party."

"You be careful, King, you hear me!" Pops stressed, pointing his fork at me. "Men are very territorial about the women that they're messing around with. They might be in a relationship and got into an argument before they came to the party."

"That's the thing, Pops. Izzy came to the party by herself. I saw ole boy walking around earlier with some tall, cute chick, so I couldn't understand why he came and asked me about Izzy. Now that I think about it… the chick was standing close by when Izzy and dude were talking."

Pops lifted an eyebrow at me and sucked his teeth.

"Do me a favor, King, and make sure you're not getting yourself in a messed-up situation. I would hate to have to fuck up someone about you," Pops said sternly.

"Pops, you don't have to worry about nothing," I assured him. Red, my grandfather's driver, walked up to the table.

"Sam, we need to leave," said Red, standing next to me. "What's up, King?" He dapped me up, and I looked over at my grandfather.

"It always seems like time flies when you're having fun." Pops sighed. "I'm sorry, King, but I need to get back to Long Beach so I can handle some business."

"They're down their tripping again?" I asked.

"Naw, it's nothing like that. I'm in the process of relinquishing a few spots over to Cash," he explained. "Are you sure you don't want to come into the candy business?"

I looked at him, smiling.

"I'm sure. We'll let Cash have it," I replied confidently.

Being a drug dealer was never an option for me because my dad was already rich when I was born. I had a trust fund set up, and I could live off of that for the rest of my life along with any children I had. If I was being honest, I was subject to inherit all of my grandfather's fortune, and that would take care of generations of little Kingdoms.

"I'll call you later to see what you have going on for tonight."

"Bet that," Pops replied. "And give some thought to what we've discussed. Maybe Izzy might be involved in too much for you right now. I think you should concentrate on graduating and fucking random women."

"Speaking of which," I said, looking at my watch. "I'm supposed to be meeting up with this little Asian and black thang when we finish lunch. Let me give her a call so I can go knock her down real quick."

"You're a chip off the old block," Pops gloated. "Don't forget to strap up."

"No doubt, Pops," I replied. "I'm not trying to have my dick burning, and I'm definitely not trying to have any kids."

TEN

Izzy

I WOKE up feeling sexually frustrated and annoyed. I couldn't believe that I attacked Kingdom like that, and of all places his mother's curtains! What the hell was I thinking... or was I thinking at all? I should have taken his ass into the bathroom. That way, old Duchess wouldn't have found us. Her precious boy was about to nut all over himself and fuck up his underwear.

I got out of the bed and headed to the shower. I cleansed my face then brushed and flossed my teeth before I got into the shower. I couldn't help but think about King and that big ass dick between his legs. My hand journeyed down to my nipple, pinching it lustfully as I thought about his thick full lips pressed against mine. There was no telling what would have happened next—maybe me bent over getting hit from the back by King. That would have been wonderful right about now.

I continued to think about my tryst in the curtains while the water from my shower rained down on my head. My center was tingling something fierce as my hand went down in between my legs and my fingers brushed against my clit. I made a mental note to get waxed because I could feel the stubble when my hand touched my pelvis. Continuing to play with my pleasure box, my body tingled with ecstasy because it felt too damn good. My thoughts were running wild, and I could feel Kingdom's breath against my skin. I thought about how he made me feel in that moment, and that's when I came.

My body slightly shook as the euphoric feeling encased my being. My center radiated an intense vibration throughout my body, and all I could do was lean against the wall. The mood quickly tanked because I saw Craig's body wash sitting on the shelf in my shower. Before I knew it, I was grabbing the bottle and opening the shower door. I attempted to throw it in the trash, but instead, it bounced off the wall, spilling all over the floor. *Fuck me!*

Jack called me to the office because the intern had messed up yet another shoot. I had a system to my madness, and I thought it was easily comprehended. It was the intern's job to pull the items and put them in a dress bag so that Jack could go through it and check it off the list. If everything was correct, then Jack either took it to the shoot, or we sent it by our courier. I called myself covering all of the bases so that I didn't have to be worried about certain mishaps, but the dumb broad that Jack picked to intern for us was the worst. I wondered if she knew how to read or comprehend. Honestly, I didn't understand why she couldn't get it. There were pictures outside of all of the shoeboxes, and she had pictures of each piece that went with the outfit. I had my clothes separated and marked by designer, and the accessories were kept in drawers that had pictures outside of them. Again, why couldn't this ditsy chick get it right?

Jack was going off on Christine, and he was tearing her a new one, which was pissing me off because he was the one who chose her to work for us. Did he not call her references or do the intern test to see if she was capable and qualified?

"Jack, stop talking to her like that," I instructed, walking past them.

"Good morning, boss," Jack replied. "You're lucky Izzy just saved you because I told her how you messed up yet again."

"I'm sorry, Jack. I thought I put all of the right items in the bag," Christine explained. "I took the pictures and called myself paying attention. I guess I got confused because there were several brown skirts on the rack."

"That might be true, boo, but there is only one brown Kate Spade skirt back there on the rack—"

"And because of that statement, Christina, I'm sorry, but your internship here with us is over," I said, interrupting Jack. "I can't accept you constantly messing up the process. This look was supposed to be couriered over to my client an hour ago for her to try it on. She has a television interview in a few hours, and she wanted to have everything at her house early."

"I'm so sorry, Izzy," Christine apologized.

"Yes, you are sorry, boo kitty," Jack scoffed, rolling his eyes. "I selected you because you had on a pair of the fiercest crocodile loafers on at your interview. The cashmere sweater you wore paired with the pencil skirt and pearls screamed sophisticated and classy. However, your skills are pathetic and unprofessional."

"What's unprofessional is you standing here berating the poor girl," I countered. "You should take some of the responsibility because you were the one who selected her to work here off of an outfit."

Jack cut his eyes at me, rolling them.

"I guess," Jack scoffed, throwing his hand up in the air. "How was I supposed to know that the poor girl couldn't read? I thought reading was fundamental, but this girl is absolutely unfamiliar. I mean, how are you graduating from college, and you can't even match up pictures with the actual items?"

"I think you should give me another chance," Christina uttered in a whiny voice. "This is the fourth internship that I've had, and I don't know if my advisor will keep approving me for them."

Staring at poor Christina, she was on the verge of a meltdown. I didn't want to seem like a mean person, but I couldn't have her fucking up my schedule either.

"Don't you dare give her another chance," Jack insisted when he saw the look on my face. "We're going to be right back here in a few hours because there's still looks that need to be put together. You know we have Duchess McDaniels coming in tomorrow, and we have over twenty looks to prepare for her."

"Damn! I almost forgot that I'm supposed to have lunch with Athlon at her house today. She's going to donate a couple of pieces of jewelry to me for the shoot," I said, feeling frustrated. I looked at my watch and pinched my temples. "Jack, you're going to have to hold Christine's hand and help her pull everything together."

"What?" Jack shouted. "I have a bunch of stuff that I have to do myself. I have to confirm the hair and makeup team that's doing this week's shoots, and I'm personally taking care of Duchess's looks. How am I supposed to do all of my work and her work too?" I looked at Jack with an annoyed look on my face. "Don't look at me like that, Izzy. You know I hate that look."

"So stop being a whiny baby, and do what I asked you to do," I fussed. "I'm the one who's going to get Duchess's stuff together. I told you that yesterday when you tried to fast-talk me into letting you do it. I told you to make sure that Jaxon B's looks are ready for tomorrow, and I hope you have them together."

"I... I... I..." Jack said, stuttering nervously.

"You sound like a scratched record Jack, which means you don't have it done," I replied, lifting an eyebrow.

"That's because I've been helping that girl," Jack complained. "I'm trying to do the best that I can, but——"

"But nothing, Jack," I said, cutting him off. "If you can't handle your job, then maybe I need to replace you as well." I threw my hands in the air, hunching my shoulders for emphasis.

"That's really not necessary. I'm sorry, Izzy, for giving you a bunch of excuses, and I will do better to make sure that incompetence does her job."

"Good," I replied with a stern look on my face. "Now, get to work because we're already behind schedule for today and tomorrow. The first thing I want you to do is get that outfit out of here and down to the studio right now!"

THE DRIVE to Pasadena was a much-needed break. I had time to clear my head from the stress that ailed me on a daily basis. Jack had been leaving Christine to her own demise while he was holding court on the phone with his boyfriend, Jose. If Jack's ass kept playing with me, he was going to have more than enough time to talk with Jose because his ass was going to be unemployed!

The gated community where Athlon lived was beautiful. There were a variety of large expensive houses with pricey cars parked in the driveways. The GPS guided me right to her house after signing in with the guard. Athlon and Chess were doing well for themselves because having a guard sign you into the community said a whole hell of a lot.

Pulling up into their driveway, I parked behind a red Range Rover. I was hoping that Athlon had prepared us some normal food because sometimes, when people have arrived, they tend to be so extra.

Don't ask Athlon any questions about Kingdom, I kept telling myself, ringing the doorbell. I had stopped by a bakery that I loved on Hollywood Boulevard and got us some of my favorite cookies. It was a lemon shortbread cookie with a light lemon frosting wash across them. I could eat an entire dozen by myself in one sitting if I'd been smoking weed. The joint I smoked on the ride over here had me hungry as a hostage, and the cookies almost didn't make it.

"Izzy, I'm so glad that you could make it to lunch," Athlon said excitedly.

"I'm glad also," I replied, hugging her. "I was up to my elbows in work when I texted you. The intern that I hired is horrible, and I want to fire her so bad."

Athlon moved out of the way and welcomed me into her home.

"So, why haven't you fired her?" Athlon asked, shutting the big wooden door behind us.

"Because I felt sorry for her," I admitted. "She said that this was her fourth internship, and she might not be able to get another one."

"That's not your problem, Izzy."

"I know, but I felt so sorry for her. She looked so pitiful, and I couldn't bring myself to do it."

"I have three women and a man that work with me at my shop. They've been with me since I started my jewelry line, and I'm so grateful to have them," Athlon replied. "My cook prepared our lunch. I hope you don't mind, but I wanted to keep things light."

"What do you mean by light?" I replied, turning my nose up. Athlon laughed at how I was looking at her, and I could tell that she was amused.

"She's preparing a crusted smoked salmon with lemon, garlic couscous, and a salad with mixed greens," Athlon explained.

"I can get jiggy with that," I replied, smiling. "I love smoked salmon, so you don't have to worry about me picking through my food."

"I see some things never change. I remember how you used to complain about the food on campus. Starting the petition to close the café down was epic."

"I swear to God, Athlon, they were trying to kill us," I said, and we both laughed.

"But you have to agree that they made the best chili cheese fries on campus."

"They did," I agreed. "I remember how the heartburn used to tear my ass up, but I wouldn't stop eating them."

"Those were the days, weren't they?" Athlon said, smiling at me.

"Yes they were," I replied. "And I'm glad that we were able to reconnect."

Athlon looked at me warmly, reaching out for a hug. Embracing her, I squeezed Athlon tightly because I missed her so much.

"Who is this strange woman you're hugging?" Chess asked, walking into the room.

"It's just some stranger that wandered in here off of the street," Athlon replied, laughing.

"Bizzy Izzy, tell me something good," Chess said happily.

"The price of pussy is down, but the stock market is steady crashing," I replied jokingly. We all laughed because Chess used to say that in college whenever someone spoke to him. He gave me a tight hug, and I felt like I was in college all over again.

"I see after all of these years you remember my old line," Chess said amused.

"Why would I forget something like that? I heard it over and over for three years. I should remember it," I countered. "I'm so happy to see you guys."

"And we're happy to see you too," Athlon acknowledged. "I hope you're not starving because it's going to be another twenty minutes before lunch is ready. What is that you have in the bag?" I looked down at it, smiling when she mentioned it.

"My fault, girl. I stopped and bought some cookies for dessert from one of my favorite bakeries on Hollywood Boulevard," I replied, looking down at the bag.

"She brought cookies, Chess," Athlon mocked, and Chess looked at her smugly.

"What's wrong? Did I do something wrong?" I asked, staring at them stupidly.

"No, of course not," Chess assured me. "It's just that Athlon is on a diet, and she's not supposed to have any baked goods. That includes cakes, cookies, pies, and pastries."

"That's all of the good shit," I scoffed, frowning. "That's why I keep my ass in the gym so that I don't get fat."

"Oh, it has nothing to do with me gaining weight. I'm pregnant and a borderline diabetic. The doctor has me on a strict diet, and the warden has been on me, making sure I eat properly."

We all laughed at her comment, but I noticed Chess looking a bit uncomfortable.

"Well, I'm not supposed to be eating these cookies either. I'm a diabetic, and I have to check my sugar several times a day."

"So, I'm just going to take these bad boys off of your hands then," Chess said, walking up to me. He held out his hand, and I gave him the bag.

"Now, I'm going to need about two of those before I leave, Chess," I said frankly. "And I'm willing to fight you for them."

He looked at me, laughing.

"These must be some good cookies," he said, looking down in the bag.

"They are," I replied. "And I will take you down if you try not to share them."

ELEVEN

King

"YOU ARE SO DISRESPECTFUL," I said, grabbing Aoi by the waist. "Scoot your ass down to the edge of this bed and put that butt up in the air."

"You're so large, King, and it's hurting," Aoi whined.

"I don't give a fuck about any of that shit you're talking. You were the one who asked for the dick, so I'm going to give it to you," I replied, rubbing the head against her wetness. "Now, take a deep breath and hold it while I put this cold muthafucka in that tight little twat."

Aoi took a deep breath as I eased the head inside of her. Letting out the breath, she moaned as I worked the head in and out of her.

"I'm going to be nice and just give you a little bit," I said, working my dick slowly, but after a few minutes, I couldn't take the pressure. I pushed as much of my dick inside of her that would fit. I was working her insides relentlessly and didn't care how much she cried out in pain.

"I can't take it, King. Please, slow down," Aoi pleaded.

"Are you sure that's what you want, Aoi?" I asked, slowing down. Pulling back, I worked the head inside of Aoi, making her purr like a kitten.

"I can stop if you want me to." Reaching down, I started rubbing her clit with my fingers while continuing to stroke and play with her money spot until I felt her muscles tighten around my rod.

"I'm about to cum," she moaned.

"I know. Give it to me," I replied, chuckling. I sped up, pushing more of me inside of her. I put both of my hands on her hips, speeding up my pace while her orgasm spread through her like wildfire. I beat her pussy up while she was screaming bloody murder, but fuck that… I was going to get my money too. Pumping inside of her a couple of more times then pulling out, I released my contents into the condom. I refused to let a chick get me caught up, and this one in particular would definitely not be seeing me anymore.

I went to the bathroom to wash myself off. Checking my messages, I saw that my mother was trying to get in contact with me. I didn't feel like being bothered with her, but I listened to her voice message just in case it was something important. Ma asked about going with her to Izzy's studio for her photoshoot, and a smile came across my face at the thought of seeing Izzy because we had some unfinished business to take care of. Miss James owed me a nut, and I had every intention on cashing in on it.

THE LAKERS WERE IN TOWN, and I wanted to go to the game. Chess had season passes that were courtside seats, and I needed to go holler at him to see if I could either take them off his hands or go with him. The Lakers were playing the Celtics, and I wanted to see Jason Tatum. That boy was nice on the court, and I wanted to see that live and in living color. I was pretty disappointed with this morning, and I didn't really enjoy having sex with Aoi. I mean, it was crazy when you enjoyed getting a hand job over being knee deep inside some pussy. I should have known her tall ass couldn't take the dick. Her camel toe wasn't even big, and that said a lot about a woman.

Pulling up in Chess's driveway, I noticed a Jeep Wrangler sitting in the driveway. The license plate caught my eye because it said

DRESSUP. It was probably one of Athlon's clients, so I didn't give it anymore thought. Pulling up next to it, I got out of my car, and my phone vibrated in my pocket. I took it out to see who was calling me, and it was Aoi. I couldn't figure out for the life of me why she was calling my line. I had just left her house over forty-five minutes ago, so she had no reason to be calling. Pressing the ignore button as I continued toward the door, I rang the doorbell while adjusting my clothes and waiting for their housekeeper to answer, but to my surprise, Chess opened it. Looking at him smiling, I pushed my sunglasses up on my head. My dreads were pulled back into a ponytail, so they slid up there with no problem.

"What's up, bruh?" I said with a big smile on my face.

"What's up, King?" he replied a bit surprised. "Were we supposed to meet up today, and I forgot about it?"

"Naw, bruh. I was in the neighborhood and decided to stop by."

"You must want something, little brother," Chess said, laughing.

I gave him some dap and a hug before he moved out of the way so that I could come inside. We walked into the living room, and I sat down on the couch. Chess sat down on the one next to me and started tying up his shoes.

"Aye, black man... can't a brother come see his big brother without needing something?" I asked nonchalantly. Chess looked at me accusingly. "Okay, Chess, I do want something, but now that I think about it, I do need to speak with you about something."

"What's up?" Chess asked. "I was about to go for a run, and the way you're dressed, you look like you could join me."

"That sounds like a good idea because I need to get the rest of this energy out of me. I just came from over this chick's house, and she pissed me off. The broad kept whining about my dick being too big, and it completely fucked up the mood."

Chess looked at me crazy then started laughing heartily.

"You crack me up, little brother, for real," Chess said entertained. "You know you like spreading your dick around like the Great Samuel Crest."

"God didn't bless me with a big dick for nothing," I scoffed. "Pops says that it's a gift that should be shared with any fine ass woman that wants to jump on it. However, I am selective about who I smash. You can't give the dick to everyone."

"That's true," Chess replied, getting up from the couch. "And you can't sex all women the same because it will cause problems in the long run. Now, c'mon let's go."

"Okay, but wait a minute. I have to get my running shoes out of the trunk," I replied, standing up. "Where's the wife?"

"She's in her studio showing one of our old college friends some of her jewelry. As a matter of fact, Izzy's going to be the one styling Duchess for her magazine shoot. That's why she's here, to pick out some jewelry."

"Izzy's here?" I asked in a panic, which I don't understand why I reacted in such a manner. "I mean…" I took a deep breath, swallowing hard. "Izzy's here at your house. Why didn't you tell me when I first arrived? Is that her jeep out front?"

Chess looked at me with a strange expression on his face. I didn't know whether to put my hands on my hips or just stand casual, and for the life of me, I didn't know why I was acting like this in the first place.

"What's wrong with you?" Chess asked in a concerned voice. "I've never seen you act like this before about a woman. How do you know Izzy anyway?"

"How am I acting?" I asked, trying to change the subject. "I mean, I was just caught off guard." I felt it was best for me to go get my running shoes, but I wanted to go steal a kiss from Izzy first. "You know what Chess? I need to use the bathroom before we leave."

I walked off in the direction of the kitchen because it was by the hallway where Athlon's studio was located. I went into the bathroom to check myself in the mirror. I was looking like my normal fine self, so I knew that baby girl wasn't going to be able to resist me. Looking down and adjusting my package in my grey sweatpants made me smile. Izzy needed to see her soon to be new best friend because of the way she was gripping this muthafucka when we were stuck in the curtains. She was going to have to finish what she started because I wanted to see what Izzy was about.

I flushed the toilet and washed my hands before exiting the bathroom. I looked around to see if Chess was lingering in the kitchen, but I didn't see him. The cook was the only one in there, and she was preparing lunch, so I made a beeline to Athlon's studio.

Slowly moving to the door, it was cracked. They were having a conversation about a necklace that was sitting on a neck form, and I couldn't help but notice Izzy's little onion butt looking good in the leggings that she was wearing. My hands started contracting because they remembered gripping that muthafucka last night, and they instantly wanted to gravitate into the studio toward her.

"Why are you peeking through the door like a stalker?" Chess asked, walking up behind me. I quickly turned around and stared at him. That's when I heard the sweet sounds of Izzy's voice.

"It seems like we have company," Izzy said, staring toward the door.

"Who is that? Chess, are you being nosy?" Athlon called out.

"No. For some reason, King is the one spying on y'all through the crack in the door," Chess explained, walking around me and pushing the door open. He went into the studio, and my back was to everyone, but I took a deep breath, turning around to face the ladies.

"What's up, everybody?" I said, casually walking into the studio. "How's my fave sister-in-law doing with my little nephew in your stomach?"

"I'm doing fine, King, and we don't know if it's a boy yet," Athlon replied, giggling.

"I know my brother knocked a boy up in there, so quit playing." I chuckled, teasing her.

Izzy was standing next to her, and I smiled warmly at her. She returned the smile, and my dick got hard in a split second. I took a step to the side to get it off my leg, but then Izzy's eyebrow lifted.

"Boy, what's wrong with you?" Athlon asked with a confused look on her face. "Put that thing up! You're embarrassing me in front of my friend."

I put my hands in front of my crotch while Izzy and Chess looked on laughing.

"You'll have to forgive my little brother," Chess apologized. "Women in leggings seem to have a strange effect on him."

"I just think that's King," Izzy replied, licking her lips. She bit down on the bottom one and gave me the same look from last night.

"You know King?" Athlon asked surprised.

"Yeah... we know each other. We've met on a few occasions. He came to my studio with Duchess for our meeting. Also, he kept me company for a while last night while trying my best to avoid Craig."

I wanted to say, "you're not going to tell them about you jacking me off in the curtains," but I decided against it. They didn't need to know our business because I was trying to have her finish today... in their house as a matter of fact.

"I saw him at the party last night, but wasn't he with some young chick?" Athlon asked.

"Yes, child," Izzy replied. "We're still in a situation, but that shit is about to be over. I'm too old to be playing games with a middle-aged man who doesn't know what he wants. I've been dating, but no one has piqued my interest." She took her gaze off of Athlon, looking at me. "It's nice to see you again, King."

"The pleasure's all mine," I replied, grinning. "Have you seen any good curtains lately?" I had to throw that in to let her know I hadn't forgotten about that situation.

"But what I want to know is why you left without saying good-bye? My mama was wondering where you had slipped off to."

"I had too much to drink, and I was afraid that I might do something that would lead to regret later," Izzy replied.

"Oh really?" I replied, wondering why would she regret it? That shit felt so good to me, and I was right there about to bust when my mama called me. "It seems like you were really enjoying yourself. I know I was enjoying myself."

Chess and Athlon were looking at Izzy and I, trying to figure out what we were talking about.

"I have to admit that it was entertaining, but I got thrown off my game. You know how that goes," Izzy said, smiling.

"What the hell are you two talking about?" Chess asked,

sounding confused. Izzy and I looked at him with the same confused expression on our face.

"We're talking about the party, bruh," I replied, staring at him.

"Remember, we mentioned that Craig was there with his thot, and it completely ruined the rest of the night for me. I poured a glass of wine on his shirt, and can you believe he left a message telling me that he's going to send me the dry cleaning bill?" Izzy scoffed, frowning.

I liked the way she thought quickly on her toes. I was going to have to watch her ass if we messed around because that meant she was good at lying.

"Oh okay," Chess replied still looking confused. "Well, King and I are about to go jogging. Come on, little brother."

"Wait a minute," I said, trying to think of an excuse to get out of running. My phone started ringing, and it completely threw me off. Pulling my phone out of my pocket, I looked at it. It was that chick again, which really pissed me off. This bitch was a straight bug-a-boo, and I was going to have to block her ass.

"Are you going to answer your phone?" Chess asked curiously.

"Naw... it's no one important." I said, shaking my head from side to side for emphasis. "Uh, Izzy, my mother's photoshoot is tomorrow, right?"

"Yes sir. I think I picked out a few good pieces that she'll like. I think I have a good idea of her style," Izzy replied confidently.

"As long as it's expensive, it's her style," Athlon mumbled.

"Huh..." Izzy uttered. Athlon looked around at everyone and put her hand up to her chest. "Oh... I have a few business suits and some classic dresses picked out for Duchess. Her name alone is a strong, bold statement."

"My mother is a whole hot mess," I said nonchalantly. "Ma is bougie and thinks that her shit don't stank. They won't tell you that in my presences, but I'm not in denial about my mother. I love her with all of my heart, but she's a piece of work."

"Words out of your mouth to God's ear," Chess said, chuckling. "Well, come on, King, so that I can get this run in. I have tickets to tonight's Laker game, and I need to take a nap before I start getting ready."

"That's why I came over here. Can I mob with you?" I asked enthusiastically.

"Sure. Dad and Pops are coming too," Chess mentioned.

"And you didn't think to invite me?" I asked, feeling offended.

"I'm sorry, King," Chess apologized. "I would have called you when I realized I left you out."

"That's cold blooded, brother," I said, sounding disappointed. We all laughed, and Izzy's pretty, pearly white teeth were showing. That was another good attribute to add to my list of positive qualities. "It was nice seeing you again, Izzy. Hopefully, we'll get to catch up soon."

"It was nice seeing you too, King," she replied pleasantly.

"Athlon," I said, smiling at her.

"Bye, King," Athlon replied, smiling back. We left the room, and thoughts of sexing Izzy were on my mind. I could see her hard nipples through that tight ass t-shirt she had on, and I was sure she took note that Coltrane was on semi against my leg. I was going to that photoshoot tomorrow with my mama, and Miss James was going to have to explain to me when she was going to finish what she started.

TWELVE

Izzy

I WASN'T EXPECTING to see King today, and it actually was rather entertaining. I couldn't believe he was questioning me like I was his girl or something. It was cute that he was spying on us through the cracked door. I wondered how long was he standing out there? My first instinct was to fall on the floor and throw my legs over my head when I saw his dick print through those grey sweatpants. It didn't look all the way hard either, but I wanted to go feel it to make sure. That was the inner hoe in me, and I must admit that I used to be a dick bandit, but my older self had slowed down when I started messing with Craig because I couldn't afford to have my walls stretched out. I wanted to be a married lady once in this lifetime.

My lunch with Athlon was enjoyable, and the pieces that I got from her were beautiful and classic. I got three necklaces, four pairs of earrings, four bracelets, and two rings. Some of them were versatile, so I could use them interchangeably. A part of me wanted to hang around a little longer to see King before I left, but I really needed to get back to the office, and it was going to take me about thirty minutes or so to get there, but the traffic on 110 was crazy at this time of the day. We'd probably be sitting on the freeway with a bunch of stupid people blowing their horns and cussing.

I pulled up in front of my office and got instantly annoyed. Craig was standing outside my studio on the phone, and I guessed he was there to bring me the receipt for his shirt. I hated a petty nigga and sometimes, the question of why I ever mixed business with pleasure came to mind. It wasn't always like this between us, but lately my patience for him had been very short. We were either going to have to come to some conclusion, or I was going to have to cut him loose.

I got out the Jeep and picked my purse up off the floor. I shut the door and moved around to the back to get the box out of the backseat. My thoughts were wandering because I didn't know what his ass was on, and I didn't feel like dealing with his bullshit.

"Let me help you with that, Izzy," Craig said, walking around to the back of the Jeep. "Why do you always insist on carrying boxes and stuff? That's why you employ that fairy and your other employees." He took the box out of my hand and shut the door. I looked at him and smiled because he called Jack a fairy.

"Don't talk about Jack. He would consider it a compliment if you called him that to his face. You know that we both are fairies though, right?"

Craig looked at me, laughing. He tried to lean in and kiss me on the lips, but I turned my head, walking away from him, hitting my alarm on my key fob.

"That was cold what you just did," Craig said, following me.

"You know we don't kiss, Craig, since you mess with Yoshi. I don't know where that girl's lips been, and I don't know where yours been either. Far as I know, you could have just ate her ass or something."

"You're being silly, Izzy," he said, sounding offended. "I just left my office, for your information." Pushing my key into the door and opening it, I pulled the knob and held it while Craig walked inside. I came in behind him and let the door close on its own.

"Izzy!" Jack called out, waving his hand. "That worthless ass Cra…" Jack stopped talking when he saw Craig standing beside me. "Hmph…" Jack scoffed, rolling his eyes. "Izzy that worthless ass nigga Craig was just here for you. Oh, Craig! I didn't see you standing right there."

"Fuck you, Jack!" Craig hissed, shoving the box he was carrying into Jack's chest. "Make yourself useful instead of running those booty eating ass lips." Jack cocked his head to the side, staring at Craig in disbelief.

"Uuhhh… nigga please don't act like you don't eat ass because I've seen you all up in Izzy's cakes before, boo kitty. Don't get cute with me, dear heart, because I will read through all of your shade and decode the message like Laura Craft, bitch."

"Yo' mama had a bitch," Craig shot back.

"Why yes she did, and I'm glad you recognize it," Jack replied, smacking his lips.

"The two of you need to cut it out right now," I insisted. My other three employees stopped working just to laugh at the petty argument that they were having. "Jack, can you please go set those up in the accessory room for me, please?"

"Yes, I can," Jack replied, fluttering his eyes. "You have a few messages from Duchess and another one from King." I looked at Jack intrigued, and he winked at me with a smug smile on his face. "You know where I'll be if you need me." Jack surveyed Craig up and down rolling his eyes hard as hell at him.

"I can't stand that fairy," Craig uttered.

"Was that supposed to offend me or something?" Jack asked smugly. "I guess you see my wings, and that's why you said that." I looked at the both of them laughing.

"Come on, Craig," I said, walking off from them. "And please don't say shit to Jack."

Craig cut his eyes at Jack before walking off, but he pushed Jack, making him drop the box. Turning around on my heels, I stared at Jack when the box hit the floor. My spider senses knew Craig had done something because he had a shit-eating grin on his face. Turning back around, I started up the steps to my office, and Craig was right behind me. When we entered my office, he shut the door then walked up on me. Wrapping his arms around my waist, he started kissing me on the neck.

"Izzy, I want to apologize to you about last night. I should have spoke to you and kept it moving," Craig said in between kisses.

"What you should be apologizing for is the other night. I'm tired of being short changed by you because you can't stay up," I complained, frowning at him.

"I know baby, and I'm sorry. You know I love this brown sugar, baby," Craig apologized, turning me around. Staring into to my eyes, he studied my face for a moment. "I've been under a lot of stress for the past few weeks. Things have been a little crazy since all of these movements have begun, and people are acting paranoid about auditions and shit."

Craig grabbed the bottom of my t-shirt, lifting it up above my waist. Next, he pulled my leggings down, staring at me seductively. "I like these panties."

"You should since you bought them," I replied dryly. "But I don't know why you're trying to waste my time, Craig. I have too much to do today and don't have time to play around with you."

The statement must have triggered something within Craig because he started lowering himself to his knees. He licked my clit through my lace panties while I stared into his eyes not impressed. He took his finger, moving my panties over to the side before he slid his tongue in between the crease of goodness. Now, his head was always satisfying, but I wasn't in the mood for it. My pussy needed a good beating, and he wasn't going to be able to polish me off properly, so I didn't know why he was wasting either of our time.

Craig spread my legs, continuing to feast on my coochie, and my body was getting aroused because he did this thing with his tongue that felt amazing. I put my hand on top of his head and started humping his face slowly. Luckily, we were right by my desk because he was pressing me against it. My legs started feeling weak as he licked down the crease of my folds then brought it back up to my clit. He latched back onto it, sucking real hard making my back arch from the wonderful feeling. I couldn't move because these leggings were binding my ankles. I gripped the sides of his face with my knees squeezing when my core tingled. It spread throughout my body while I let out a soft low moan. Dropping my head back, I rode my orgasm since it was the only one I'd be getting from this jerk. There was something strange about the visit, but I couldn't quite figure it out. I knew Craig wasn't eating pussy in order to get me to pay for his shirt; at least, I don't think that's why he did it.

"Did you like that, Izzy?" Craig asked seductively licking his lips as he got up off his knees. His face still had some of my juices on it that he was wiping off as he stared at me.

"It was cool," I said slightly trembling. He looked me in the eyes, and we both started laughing. "I guess I enjoyed it a little bit, but this doesn't change the fact that I'm mad at you."

I kicked my Uggs off my feet before pulling my leggings and underwear off as well. Picking them up off the floor, I walked toward my bathroom.

"You should let me make it up to you by taking you out to dinner tonight," Craig proposed. "We can go to whatever restaurant you want, and afterward, maybe go catch some jazz or something over at the Rhythm Room."

My eyes narrowed at Craig smugly before walking into my bathroom. Grabbing a washcloth out of the basket, I stuck in the sink, turning on the water.

"I don't know, Craig, because I have a long day ahead of me tomorrow. I mean dinner sounds nice, but going to a jazz spot afterward is going to be too much," I replied, grabbing the soap. I lathered up the washcloth and began cleaning myself off while Craig was continuing to press the issue of going out tonight.

"We can cut out the jazz club and just go back to my house and cuddle. You used to like to just cuddle up in bed with me, Izzy. What happened that you're suddenly obsessing about our sex life? Does it have anything to do with that young dude at the party? Duchess's son... what's his name?" Craig questioned, sounding annoyed.

"What do mean?" I scoffed, frowning. What the fuck did King have to do with anything? "I was perfectly fine with cuddling with you, Craig, but here and now lately, that's all that we do. Also, I don't know what King has to do with any of this, but you can stop barking up that tree because it's nothing there." At least that's all Craig needed to know.

"The two of you looked real cozy last night, and he acted real smug when I tried to ask about you," Craig said waiting for my response. I continued to clean myself up and wasn't going to feed into the King comment.

"Izzy, I told you that I was stressed out. What part of that don't you understand?" Craig replied with an attitude. I cut the water off and threw the washcloth into the dirty clothes hamper where I put the leggings and thong.

"You know what, Craig, thank you for the invitation, but I'm cool," I replied coming out the bathroom. He stared at me because I didn't have anything on the bottom half of my body.

"Are you going to put something on?" he asked with an attitude.

"Are you going to put something on?" I mocked, walking over to my closet and opening the door. I went into the container where my clean underwear was kept. I pulled out a yellow thong and put it on. "Why does it bother you that I'm naked? If I don't care, then I don't understand why you're so bothered by it."

"What if one of your employees come up here and sees you?" Craig replied frankly.

"I don't give a fuck about them seeing my pussy. I'll walk downstairs just like this, and it wouldn't phase a soul. We have naked women and men walking around here all the time. We're not embarrassed by nudity, and one would think that your grown ass wouldn't be either."

"It's the respect factor at play here," Craig complained with his brow furrowed. "One of them can claim sexual harassment against you."

"Do you really think that Jack would say that I sexually harassed him?" I questioned inquisitively. "And for your information, Jack is the person who does my Brazilian wax."

"Jack has seen your—"

"Pussy," I said, interrupting him. "Yes, he has… several times."

I giggled and took a pair of jogging pants out of another container. I put them on and continued listening to Craig fuss about my pussy being exposed to my employees as I made my way over to my desk and sat down in my chair. The messages that Jack mentioned to me were in plain sight, so I picked them up shuffling through them until I came to the one from King. It had his number on it and said to call whenever I got the message. A smile came across my face as I thought about his full soft lips against mine. I wondered if he knew how to give good head because his lips looked and felt like pillows. Craig noticed that I wasn't paying him any attention, so he came walking over to me turning my chair around to face him.

"Are you even listening to me, Izzy?" Craig snapped. "See, this is the shit that I'm talking about. You want me to commit to you, but you can't even respect me enough to give me your undivided attention." Looking up at Craig nonchalantly, I began sighing.

"Craig, I have a lot of work to do. Thank you for the little pick me up, but if you're going to lecture me each time we're together, then I'd rather you just call me on the phone." I could see his ears turning red which meant that he was pissed at me.

"You sure are right," Craig hissed angrily. "Maybe we should cancel dinner because I don't want to further annoy you."

"I'm glad you understand, and maybe you should take Yoshi," was my suggestion.

"I think I will… at least she'll appreciate it," Craig replied before storming out of my office.

Settling my head against the back of my chair, my mood changed instantly because I didn't want things to go this way. Only if Craig could understand my point of view, then we wouldn't be having these problems.

THE NEXT DAY

A strange thing happened this morning. My thoughts were focused on seeing King at the photoshoot today, and a part of me was excited. I managed not to call the number he left for me, which I don't know why I didn't. My thoughts were focused on what happened with Craig in my office, so I couldn't have possibly held a decent conversation with King. However, today, I would try hard to be on my best behavior and not corner young King into one of my rooms and attack him.

"Good morning, queen," Jack said, walking up behind me.

"Good morning, Jack," I replied sweetly. "You know I didn't get any sleep last night. My thoughts were so focused on this photoshoot today." Walking over to the rack of dresses marked "Duchess McDaniel," I started looking at the selection of clothing.

"Are you sure your thoughts were on this photoshoot, or were they on Kingdom McDaniel? Did you call him last night?" Jack asked being his usual nosey self.

"No, I didn't call him. There was so much stuff on my mind that I wouldn't have been able to concentrate."

"Are you sure that you weren't tripping off of that head that Craig gave you in the office yesterday because I'm going to say to you, is no… ni… ni… no… no… no!" Jack shouted, swinging his head from side to side. "He is not allowed to come in here and cock block a very handsome young man that is very much interested in you, Izzy. It's high time you stop putting your life on hold for a man who obviously doesn't appreciate you."

"I know, Jack, but I have to be careful. I can't go running off with the first man that shows interest in me. Besides, King is young, and I don't want to get involved with someone who hasn't had the opportunity to live his life," I replied frankly. "The only thing that young boy can do is let me ride that big ass dick of his; speaking of which, let me tell you what happened yesterday. I was having lunch with Athlon, and guess who walked into the room?"

"Kingdom?"

"Yes! And he had on a pair of grey jogging pants."

"Oh lawd… please have mercy on my pour twisted soul," Jack declared, clutching his invisible pearls. "How was it hanging, gurl?"

"Over to the left, mid-thigh, and almost solid against his thigh," I replied, laughing. "Child… when I say my eyes were focusing on it while my mouth was watering something fierce! My insides wanted me to get down on my knees and crawl over to him like a dog with its tongue out because I wanted to suck that muthafucka."

"Why didn't you, Izzy? I'm sure Athlon would have understood that you turned into an animal on the prowl, who was fixating on their prey," Jack said, encouragingly.

"You are a fool, you know that?" I replied, laughing. "It's a damn shame that you would encourage my foolery, but I love you so much for it. I have to be realistic about the whole thing, and I think that King's fascination with me is purely sexual."

"That's great! Who said anything about a relationship, Izzy? You can fuck that young man and give him the gift of experienced vagina. It's not too often that a man gets to experience gifted vajay-jay. Isn't that what old boy from that one popular R&B group said about your pussycat? 'Thank you for letting me experience that gifted vagina.'"

We both fell out laughing because a certain celebrity, that will remain nameless, sent me flowers with those words written on a card. I used a few of my tantric moves on him, and I guess he recognized my swagger.

"I couldn't believe it when I read that shit on the card. The flowers were beautiful, though, and the trip to Napa was amazing," I admitted to Jack. "I think if I whip my superpowers on King, he's going to fall in love, and I don't know if I can handle dealing with the immaturity of a twenty-something adult male. They are weird, horny creatures, and I don't know if I'm up for the challenge."

"Bitch, you don't do yoga, pilates, and work out regularly to not be able to show your flexibility on a dick. Craig knows how to pull your card, and I can't believe a few licks on your clit is interfering with your rational thinking... but you are getting older."

"Hisssssss..." I said, throwing up my hands like a clawing cat. "Princess, get your ass over there, and get ready for Duchess's arrival. I want you to kiss that bitch's ass and make her feel like she's the Duchess of York up in this mutha."

Jack cocked his head to the side, looking at me strangely. He thought for a moment then started giggling uncontrollably.\

"You're calling me by my alias because I'm being real catty with you right now," Jack uttered. "However... you're giving me instructions and dismissing me because I'm getting on your nerves."

"Ding... ding... ding... we have a winner, folks!" I shouted, clapping enthusiastically. "I don't want to talk about this anymore right now because I have a lot of anxiety and stress going on right now. I want this photoshoot to be a success, and if I can't concentrate on the task at hand, then I could potentially destroy my business."

"I don't think it's that serious, but okay, Izzy. I'll leave it alone... for right now," Jack replied smugly. "Why don't your anxious ass go up on the roof and smoke a joint? Grab the bottle in your drawer that's marked anxiety and smoke one of those. It will calm you down and make you feel more relaxed."

"Good idea," I said, smiling at Jack. "This is how I like you, Jack... being helpful and not pushy." I cupped his face in my hand, wrinkling my nose at him and shaking my head from side to side. "I'll be on the roof. Please text me when Duchess arrives."

"Will do."

THIRTEEN

Duchess

"I'M COUNTING on you to keep King focused at all times," I instructed Chelsea. "He needs to see how intelligent you are, dear, because your beauty is obviously evident."

"Yes, ma'am," Chelsea replied, smiling. "I tried to talk with him at the party, but his attention seemed to be elsewhere."

"Well, since I'm going to be occupied with taking pictures, you can keep my boy entertained," I asserted. "If you want King to take notice of you, then you're going to have to be more aggressive in your pursuit. I think it's time for my son to settle down and make some decisions in his life and getting a beautiful, intelligent girl-friend should be his course of action. It's the best next step after college."

"I don't think King wants that," Chelsea uttered softly. "He's known around town as the sexy, flirtatious bachelor of a well-known socialite and tech company owner in Silicon Valley. Almost every single woman in LA knows the name King McDaniel, and they also know that he's not trying to be 'tied down to no woman,' his exact words." I glared over at Chelsea because it was obvious she was not really a fighter. However, she was the person I picked for King to date for right now because I hadn't found the perfect wife for him, yet.

"Chelsea, I'm not interested in what King wants right now because he doesn't have a clue about life. It is up to me to help my son make all of the important decisions for his life, and I think recommending you to date will help tip the scales in your favor."

We pulled up in front of Izzy's studio, and a chill went down my back. I saw her when she bolted out of my custom-made drapes, and King came stumbling out behind her. It took me a second to get to him, and when I did, his clothes were messy, and his face was red and flushed. He smelled of women's perfume, and his lips and neck were smeared with red lipstick. I didn't say anything to him because he was in a pissy mood when I approached him. I think something was going on between them, but I was going to nip that shit in the bud.

We walked into the studio, and the vibe was very relaxed and serene. The air smelled of vanilla, and the place had been completely transformed since the other day. There were several backgrounds strategically placed around the warehouse space. There were pieces of furniture sitting nearby and a table full of snacks with beverages on it in the distance. I must admit that I was impressed by the professionalism that was being displayed around here. There were two bottles of wine chilling in ice buckets on the table, and I knew she had me pegged. A young woman was wheeling a rack of clothes toward a room, so I figured that's where I needed to be.

"Duchess! Welcome to your photoshoot," Jack said enthusiastically as he approached us. I smiled at him warmly because he's so adorable.

"Hello, Jack," I replied pleasantly. "It looks busy around here."

"Yes, ma'am, and it's all for you," he replied smiling coyly. "I just texted Izzy, and she should be down in a second, but in the meantime, I will show you to the dressing room where you will be getting your hair and makeup done. Can I interest you in a bottled water, juice, or a glass of wine?"

"That sounds perfect, but I want to get settled in first before I get a drink," I replied. However, I wanted to know why Izzy's ass wasn't down here to greet me. "Where's Izzy?"

"Oh… she's on the rooftop meditating," Jack explained. "She likes to clear her head before she starts working."

"That sounds wonderful," I replied. "I like to meditate in the mornings after I pray."

"I use prayer as my meditation," Izzy said, walking up behind us. "Welcome, Duchess. I'm so excited about styling you today."

"Thank you, Izzy. However, I must admit that I'm a bit nervous. I don't usually let anyone make decisions for me when it comes to my clothes, but you are a professional." *And I hope she doesn't make me look stupid,* I thought in my head.

"Yes, ma'am… I am, and I promise you're going to love the clothes I've picked out for you," Izzy assured me. "I borrowed a few pieces from Dior, Channel, Kate Spade, Yves Saint Laurent, and Gucci because, in my opinion, their clothing will best represent your style."

"It sounds like you've been in my closet," I said, laughing. "I own pieces from all of them, and they're all my favorites."

"That's good to hear. I'm glad that I selected them for you," Izzy replied, smiling. "Let's get you in hair and makeup."

"I hope you don't mind, but I asked my LA hair stylist to stop by to do my hair," I mentioned because I didn't let just anyone get up in my hair.

"Well, the hair stylist that I work with does a lot of the black celebrities' hair here in LA. His name is Rico, and he even does hair shows and demonstrations for some of the major hair product manufacturers," Izzy explained.

"I had no idea that you worked with so many professionals," I replied nonchalantly.

"I told you, Duchess, I got you," Izzy assured me. "I know that us black women are very particular about who puts their hands in our hair. You have a beautiful mane of hair, and I'm sure that's because you don't let just anyone up in your head."

"You are very observant, Izzy, and I like that in you," I said, smiling happily. "I'm going to get my spoon out of your Kool Aid and let you do your job." Both Izzy and Jack laughed as I continued smiling at the both of them smugly. She better hope that I like what she's selected because I have no problem checking her if I have to.

FOURTEEN

Izzy

WHY DID I know that Duchess was going to roll up in here being extra? She gon' have a hairstylist show up at my studio and I politely dismissed her ass with the quickness. She's not going to come up in my shit and try to dismantle what the fuck I put together. She was a controlling and pushy woman, but she had me fucked up on every base on this here Saturday.

"Why hasn't she come out of the dressing room, yet?" I asked, walking over to Jack.

"I don't know, Izzy," Jack replied, looking confused. "She was complaining about the last three outfits she took pictures in, but I thought she looked beautiful."

"She did look beautiful," I agreed. "It's just that she wanted to mix match designers in a bad way, and I wouldn't let her. I wanted her to wear the light blue Dior blouse with the navy slacks, but she wanted to wear the blouse with one of the pairs of pants from the Channel suits."

"How disrespectful," Jack scoffed, rolling his eyes.

"She doesn't know any better," I replied, rolling mine too.

There was no way I was going to mix up those two designers because I assured them that I was going to use the entire garment that I borrowed from them. It's free publicity to the elite in LA, and if Duchess McDaniel is seen in a magazine wearing their fashions, it would bring customers to their shops, and I would be gifted some fabulous clothing. It's a win-win situation.

"This is more like it," Duchess fussed, fixing the sleeve of her blouse. "Chanel is my favorite."

"We know, Mother," King said, walking up behind us. "You have about twenty of her suits in your closet."

The hairs on the back of my neck stood up, and I felt my shoulders tense up. Why does that always happen to me when he speaks, and why does he keep walking up behind me like that? I never hear his ass coming.

"Son! I was wondering when you were going to get here," Duchess gushed. "Come give your mommy a kiss."

"And get all of that gunk on my lips… no thank you," King replied, frowning. "Besides, you look beautiful, Ma. I don't want to mess up your makeup." I turned around, smiling at King.

"Hi, King," I said warmly.

"Hey, Miss James," he replied and bit his bottom lip. "You look nice today, even though I really liked those leggings you had on yesterday." I blushed because that was unexpected, and I guess he noticed because he started smiling at me. The simple pink cotton dress I had on clung to my curves in all the right places, and he could slip his hand up under here if he liked.

"King, why don't you walk with me over to the set," Duchess interrupted curtly. "Did you see Chelsea?"

"Yeah… that's why it took me so long to come over here," he explained. "She was unusually chatty with me, and I found myself stuck for a few minutes talking about graduation."

"Well, you know she's graduating this year too," Duchess replied. "She'll have a degree in communications."

"What do you do with a degree in communications?" I asked.

Duchess looked over and cut her eyes at me. My head instantly moved back in shock because I didn't know where that look came from.

"She's going back to school to get her master's in broadcasting.

She wants to be a news anchor," Duchess explained smugly. "I think she has the perfect face for it, wouldn't you agree, Izzy?"

"Oh yes," I replied agreeably. "She has a beautiful face, but I hope she doesn't get any more plastic surgery because it will start to mess with her facial structure."

"Chelsea hasn't had any work done on her face," Duchess insisted.

"Ummm… yes she did," I assured her. "She told me that she had some work done on her nose and her lips."

"I had no idea," Duchess replied. "She's never mentioned that to me."

"Why would she?" King asked confused. "That's not something that people just mention in casual conversation."

"I guess you're right, King," Duchess said, giggling. "Come, son. Let's walk over here so we can get this thing wrapped up. I was hoping that we could have lunch afterward."

"I'm sorry, Mama, but I have a class in two hours that I have to go to," King said, apologizing. "But maybe I'll come out to the house to see you later." A warm smile spread across Duchess's lips, and she touched the side of King's face.

"Okay, sweet boy," she gushed.

"Ma, I'm a man," King said, looking over at me then back at her.

My heart fluttered watching their exchange because King looked so sexy in his baggy khaki chinos, a black short sleeve button up shirt and a pair of black Chuck Taylors. His hair appeared like it had just been re-twisted and it was braided back in an elaborate pinup. He was looking so damn good that I just wanted to sex him right where he stood.

We managed to get a few shots off, but Duchess kept complaining about the set. It was an office setting with a mahogany desk and brown soft leather office furniture. She felt like it was too much and kept asking if we could use another scene. King kept trying to help and that really made me take notice of him. He was encouraging his mother and kept telling her that she looked fine, but

Duchess just insisted on being extra. It didn't help that her dumb ass assistant Chelsea kept agreeing with everything that she said. I wanted to smack the shit out of her and put her out of my studio, but that wouldn't be professional. I noticed that Chelsea was standing very close to King, and he kept moving away from her, but for some strange reason, she kept gravitating back next to him. King was looking uncomfortable and at one point he told her to go get him something to drink in order to get some space. He must have noticed me watching them because when I was laughing at them, he saw me. Narrowing his eyes at me, King blew a kiss. I looked around as if I didn't know he was directing it at me, but it seemed like Duchess noticed because she instantly started calling his name.

"King, don't you think the pictures would look better against that white background," Duchess whined.

"Ma, would you stop being so difficult and take the damn pictures," King said, frowning with an annoyed look on his face. I found it refreshing how he talked to her, wishing he could've called her a bitch.

"I have an idea," I said, walking up to her. "Why don't we put King in some of the pictures with you. I have a few Brooks Brothers suits on a rack, and I'm sure I have one that would fit him. You're about a thirty-two in the waist aren't you, King?"

"Good guess, but I wear a thirty-four in the waist and a thirty-two length," King replied. "But I don't want to be in this lady's pictures." He looked at me with a frown on his face, and I want to do is walk up to him and kiss those pouty lips.

"Why not, King?" Duchess asked surprised. "You used to like taking pictures with mommy. I take those ridiculous Snapchat videos with you, and I'm always on your Instagram. Why can't you do this for me?" King looked at his mother's pitiful face and caved like a little bitch.

"Okay, Mama, but these are the only pictures that I'm taking with you," he said sternly.

"Bet, King," she replied smiling.

"I think these pictures are going to be the best ones on the roll,"

Chelsea chimed in. "King, you're going to look so handsome posing next to your beautiful mother."

I rolled my eyes at that heffa because Chelsea was trying to score some brownie points.

"King, Jack can take you over to the rack of suits to find one to fit you. I will go pull a shirt and some accessories to go with it. I think you'll look absolutely sexy in these leather braided suspenders that I have," I observed, checking his frame. "Jack can you check to see if that butterscotch suit is in King's size? I want to play off his beautiful green eyes and I think the butterscotch would go perfectly with his complexion."

"I agree," Duchess added staring at King. "You do have a good eye, Izzy."

"Why thank you, Duchess, and here I thought you didn't have faith in my talents or my vision," I replied dryly. "But wait until we incorporate King into the equation. You'll see exactly what I was going for with this look."

It was taking King a minute to come out, so my curiosity was piqued. It was not that difficult to put on a pair of pants, a shirt, some suspenders and a suit jacket, so why is he holding us up? It was my idea to put him in the dressing room on the other side of the studio and that was a good idea because I was about to do something slick.

King didn't close the door all the way and I just so happen to be strolling by when our eyes locked. He stared at me seductively and did the unthinkable. He whipped his dick out in his hand stroking it slowly. My mouth fell open as I looked around the room. Everyone seemed to be preoccupied with whatever they were doing so this girl decided to go help that young man out.

My legs were moving without me telling them to go. The room wasn't that big, so we would literally be on top of each other. King bit his bottom lip staring while I closed the door behind me, locking it.

"You look like you could use some help. Let me assist you." I said moving his hand out of the way and replacing it with mine. The right hand has magic and that's the one that went to work.

Slowly and calculatedly my hand moved up and down his shaft. The girth of his dick was so thick that my fingers couldn't fit around the whole thing, but that didn't stop anything.

"You like stroking dicks, huh," King said sarcastically.

"You wanted me to stroke this big muthafucka. That's why you had the door open in hopes that I walked by, so quit fronting. You like me playing with this dick," I replied nonchalantly. "But this time we're going to finish what we started."

"Bet," King uttered quickly as I continued working him in my hand. We were staring each other down and my mouth was watering while my body was getting aroused. My teeth sank down into my bottom lip because the faces King was making had a bitch weak. I licked my lips hungrily before leaning in to whisper sweet nothings into his ear.

"Eeeewwww… sssss… you feel so good in my hand," I taunted. "You want to put your dick in my wet pussy, don't you?"

"Hmmm… hmmm…" he moaned in response. "Speed up."

"Nck… nck… nck… nck…" came flowing out of my mouth. "You're not running shit here. Big Mama is in control of this. Now you're about to cum for mommy because we have some work to do. However, if you're a good little boy, maybe we can do real grown-up things later."

My hand continued to stroke him good and King was enjoying every minute of it. He grabbed the back of my head and brought my lips to his as we kissed nastily and our tongues intertwined. He was sucking on my bottom lip as my hand sped up the pace. I could feel his dick getting harder and his big vein popping out against my hand.

"Give it to me, baby… give mommy all this nut," I purred against his lips as the moment of truth was happening.

"Uhhh… uhhh… uuuuuhhhhhhh," King groaned as he released himself into the palm of my hand. Looking over to the side of us, I grabbed a few Kleenex out of the box, and I put it up to King's rod, collecting everything he had to give.

"Is that all you got for me?"

"Hell naw… but I guess it'll have to do for now," King replied laughing.

I reached my hand up to my mouth, licking some of his essence off my hand. Our eyes were in a trance with one another, and King narrowed his eyes watching me slide my fingers in and out of my mouth suggestively.

"Mmmm… you taste good, baby. Real tropical like," I teased. The way my eyes were staring at him, King knew what time it was. If we weren't on a schedule, then we would have been fucking up in that dressing room. However, work always comes first, but we'd have our time and you could take that to the bank.

THE PHOTOS WERE AMAZING that King took part in today. He really shined and looked so sexy doing it. His presences made everything better, and I was impressed at how photogenic he was when the photographer gave him directions. What people don't understand is just because you're cute doesn't mean you'll take good pictures. I've seen plenty of cute girls bomb a photoshoot. The way King wore that suit made me think about undressing him slowly in his office and fucking him senseless on his desk. It was interesting how his gaze stayed on me the entire time, and I think Miss Chelsea picked up on it because she came and stood right next to Jack and me.

Walking past Duchess's dressing room, I overheard she and Chelsea talking about King. Now, I shouldn't have been nosy, but my curious ass had to hear what they were talking about. Like I said before, it was confusing when Chelsea came over to where I was standing and set up camp. King was watching me and I was watching him, and it just so happened that my tongue kept licking my lips with my eyes staring at his package. I would draw up my nose up when a pose didn't look right, or I'd bite my bottom lip when I was totally digging what he was doing. We were having a nonverbal conversation with one another that only we understood.

Surveying the clothes on the rack was a good cover for my ear hustling in on the women's conversation because they were speaking rather loudly. Duchess was doing most of the talking, but Chelsea would chime in when it was appropriate. I thought it was rather strange, but Chelsea was Duchess's assistant.

"I'm pleased with how things turned out," Duchess said proudly. "Having King in my photographs made them that much better."

"I agree," Chelsea replied. "But did you see the way that King and Izzy were staring at each other. If I didn't know any better, I would swear that they were flirting with one another."

"I did notice that Izzy's face was a bit overly exaggerated at times during the shoot, but I didn't see what you're talking about. Besides... she's way too old for King, and he doesn't like older women."

"What do you mean?" Chelsea asked, interested in what she had to say. "Because I heard a rumor around school that he's having sex with his counselor, Sarah Dexter."

A gasp came out of my mouth when I heard Chelsea say that to Duchess. He's fucking one of the administrators at the university. That's way too much information.

"What are you talking about?" Duchess snapped with an attitude. "My son wouldn't dare do something like that... would he? King does have a lot of his grandfather's traits in him. Also, he's good at seducing women. I watched him talk a hostess into getting us a table immediately when there was a thirty-minute wait. However, what does that have to do with anything? King's not interested in Elizabeth James. He's just being friendly and polite because he knew I was worried about looking good for the photoshoot."

I had heard enough and walked away from the door. He's just like Sam? Lord knows I don't want to get involved with him if that's the case. I'd rather take my chances with Craig instead of entertaining all of that foolishness. Jack said just have sex with King, but my ass would end up falling in love with him, and my heart couldn't take it if things went bad between us. I'd be jealous and watching his every move; no not I said the little bird. This girl refused to be apart of his chain of fools. However, my pussy said 'girl, forget all of that bullshit and let that young nigga bust it wide open. You know you liked it when his dick was in your hand. It's long overdue, Izzy'. *Calm down, hormones,* my brain told my coochie. King was way too young for me anyway, and I needed to focus on this mess I had going on with Craig.

FIFTEEN

Izzy

CALL ME A PUNK, but I ran and hid in my office until I thought everyone was gone. I couldn't face Duchess or King because my impression of him was tarnished by the conversation I overheard. I'm very much attracted to him, but I needed to forget about him and focus on someone else. His dick was big, and it was almost in my mouth, but it would be much better this way. He got a free nut from me, and that's that.

I picked up a basket of accessories that was on my desk and walked outside of my office. It was relatively quiet, except for the normal conversations and chatter around here as I made my way down the steps, heading to the accessory closet. There was some processing that needed to happen in my head and organizing the accessory closet always helped me out.

The door was closed, so I grabbed the knob, pushing it open and it swung back toward the wall behind me. Usually, it would close on its own, so I didn't bother looking behind me to check it as I walked over to the table and set the basket on top of it, but for some reason, it fell over spilling everywhere.

"Shit!" I yelled, bending down to pick the stuff up, but when my head lifted, I damn near fell down because King was standing in front of me.

"What's the matter, Izzy?" King asked smiling lustfully at me. I had on a cowl neck shirt that hung very low, and he could see straight down into my cleavage.

"Nothing," I said, standing up and staring into his jade colored eyes. They were the prettiest color green, and I wanted to get lost in them. *Snap out of it, Izzy. You heard what Chelsea and Duchess said about you.* "I thought you guys left."

"No… we're still here," King replied, chuckling. "My mother cornered the photographer and insisted on him showing her the photos."

"Why is that not surprising?" I said, walking around him. "I thought you mentioned something about going to class."

"That was a lie I told my mother to get out of going to lunch with her and Chelsea. However, you owe me something, and we need to finish what you started from last night and today," King explained, walking up to me placing his hands on my hips and pressing his lips against mine. We kissed for a second, but I broke away taking several steps backward to catch my breath.

"You're just a baby," I said, smiling coyly at this fine little boy.

"I'm not a baby. I'm a grown ass man who knows how to do grown man things, I told you," King said confidently. He walked up to me, lifting my chin to stare down into my eyes.

Now, I knew I had no business entertaining this man-child's conversation because he was a straight up hoe. There's no way getting around it and if he's fucking his counselor there had to be more women out there, right or wrong?

I walked away trying to give myself a pep talk. *Izzy, get yourself together! You can't get involved with King.* That's what I kept telling myself, but I knew me… and I couldn't resist a fine ass man and a big dick.

"Are you bargaining with yourself right now?" King asked curiously with a coy look on his face. I had my back to him and was praying to God to give me strength. My body wants to feel him inside of me, but *'my mind's telling me no! But my body… my body's telling me yeah!'* King walked up behind me, pressing his semi hard-on against my butt. "Do I make you feel nervous?"

"Why do you say that? Was it that obvious what I was doing?" I asked sweating like a hooker in church as I glanced over my shoulder at him, chuckling nervously.

"It's very obvious, but I find it sexy," King said kissing my shoulder. "Do I turn you on, Elizabeth?" King whispered in my ear, and I felt my panties getting wet. The warmth of his breath on the back of my neck made my knees buckle, and I damn near fell on the floor. Why is he standing so damn close to me?

I turned my head to get a better look at him and caught a whiff of a sweet smell. *Damn! His breath smells like peppermints. I wonder does his tongue taste like it too? Stop it, Izzy!*

"Excuse me, King," I said, trying to move away from him again, picking up a few random bracelets sitting on table. King was amused while quietly watching me intently. I didn't know what to do because I was either on the verge of a nervous breakdown, or I was about to pull my dress up and bend over to let him hit it from the back.

"I'm going to give you some time to think about us," King said nonchalantly. I turned around quickly, and King was still smiling with his pearly whites shining.

"There is no way in hell I'm messing with a twenty-two-year-old," I said unsteadily, not sounding convincing. "I mean I'll be thirty-four this year, and I'm old enough to be your mother."

Now maybe I went a bit too far with that one, but I could have been a teenage mother because I was fast as hell. However, I absolutely can't mess with a hoe.

"Why can't you find someone your own age?" I asked him curiously.

"Because they're all stupid and superficial. The only thing they care about is buying bundles, getting their nails done and whether or not MAC is coming out with a new lip color," he complained, arrogantly.

"Wait a minute," I said staring at him with a confused look on my face. "Those are things I care about."

"Don't patronize me, Izzy. Women your age know how to do things in bed that young girls don't know about," King explained, moving my hair out of my face, looking into my eyes. "And the other night when you kissed me—"

"It was a mistake," I blurted out in a panic. "I was drunk, and I shouldn't have taken advantage of your young impressionable self."

"Let that be the reason, Izzy," King replied, chuckling. "You were definitely more relaxed that night. What happened to the woman that was just in the room jacking me off?" King moved closer to me, putting his hands on my shoulders. He began massaging them and my head instantly dropped forward because my muscles were so tense from the pressure of his mother's photo-shoot. My body was responding to him, and my center was yearning for his tongue.

Now, why did this boy have to start touching all on me? I had to mentally tell my coochie to calm down because the bitch was ready to jump out like the Predator. *We are not about to fuck this dude, so you need calm the fuck down*, I told her. I tried to move away again, but King had me pinned against the counter pushing his pelvis forward as his erection pressed against the crease of my butt.

"Do you feel that Izzy? He wants you," King whispered in my ear before planting soft kisses on my neck. He brought one of his hands up cupping my breast as he grinded his stiffness against my ass; almost making me come on myself from clothes burning.

Little baby Jesus, I need you now more than ever! Why did he have to up and put his dick on me and grind it in my ass? I liked nasty shit like this, and I was feeling so vulnerable and weak.

Before I knew it, my head was on King's shoulder and we were tonguing again. He was pinching and pulling my nipples why my ass moved against his erection. He turned me around pressing his lips right back against mine. We were kissing nastily and groping each other lustfully. He grabbed the bottom of my dress, pulling it up while my hands unfastened his pants. It was about to go down up in here and both of us were going to be very happy campers.

"Am I interrupting something?" Jack asked, walking into the accessory closet. He was looking at both of us smugly, so I knew it didn't look good. Jack clutched his pearls while staring at me accusingly. I quickly moved away from King, but not before I looked down at his package. My mouth was watering, and I wanted to put Jack out so I could drop down to my knees and kill myself from choking off of his dick. However, I owed Jack a debt of gratitude because he saved me from myself.

"No, you're not disturbing anything, Jack. We were just in here talking," I replied, looking sweaty and a bit flushed.

"You two looked mighty cozy to me if you were just talking, boo kitty," Jack said sarcastically. "It looked like you were drooling, so I guess that can count for something." Jack smirked at me before rolling his eyes.

I couldn't stand Jack's ass at times because he was always observing some shit and calling me on it. He plays all day, and he didn't even have to bust me out like that.

"Well, I'm about to go find my folks," King announced, adjusting himself. Jack and I stared at him lustfully, and I elbowed Jack when I saw him gawking at King.

King came over to me and planted a firm kiss in the middle of my forehead and pulled away looking at me with a pleasant smile on his face. He walked away and when he made it to the door, he stopped and turned to face me.

"We're definitely going to have to finish this some other time. I'm a patient man, and my mama didn't name me Job for nothing," he said winking at me, walking out of the door. Jack looked at me with shock on his face and I was left speechless.

"Biiiiiiiiiittttttttcccccccccchhhhhhhh!" Jack called out. "Did that dude just tell you that he's going to wait on the pussy?"

"Baaaaby… I am outdone," I said fanning myself. "Thank you for saving me because I almost fell weak."

"Uhhh… huh…" Jack signified. "That boy had your ass hemmed up in this muthafucka!" We both laughed hard because he was telling the truth.

"I need to tell you the conversation I overheard between Duchess and Chelsea. That way you'll understand why I'm cool on

Kingdom McDaniel, and maybe you'll back up off of me about messing with him."

"So, spill the tea gurl so I can be in on the brunch, and I don't have all day," Jack said in a catty manner.

"How about we go get dinner and a drink. I think we deserve it after the day we've had leading up to this photoshoot and afterward," I suggested.

"Let me call my bae so he can meet us," Jack said, pulling out his phone. "You know he goes crazy when I go out without him."

"That's fine. You can call him while I go upstairs and take a shower. I need to go work some things out because that boy has got me all worked up. My panties are literally wet," I teased. However, I wasn't playing because he really did something to me.

SIXTEEN

King
___

IZZY LOOKED SO DAMN good today. I wanted to sex her long and hard in that little room, but I had to control myself. We needed to finish what she started earlier, and I'm going to show up at her studio every day until she agreed to give me some of that goodness.

"King, are you still coming over for dinner? I'll have Chelsea pick up your favorite dessert, and we can have an intimate dinner on the patio just you, Chelsea, daddy, and I," Duchess said, smiling at me.

"Ma, I got plans with Pops, and I need to get to school," I said before kissing her on the cheek. "I'll try to stop by after class, but I'm not going to make any promises." My feet carried me to my car expediently, and I jumped inside with the quickness. I was tired of her trying to make Chelsea my chick, and I was just going to have to talk to her about that.

I started my car and texted my mother a message. I told her to stop trying to force Chelsea on me. She instantly texted me back and tried to play dumb like she didn't know what I was talking about. I threw my phone into the cup holder because that shit pissed me off. I needed to get home to take a shower and get myself ready for tonight.

I WIPED the mirror off and stared at my reflection. The stubble on my face gave me a more mature look, so shaving was out of the equation for tonight. I decided to wait until tomorrow because I liked this look on me. I put on some deodorant and sprayed some Gucci Guilt against my bare skin. I didn't like putting cologne on my clothes because that shit could fuck up a shirt.

It was time to get ready as I stood in my walk-in closet staring at my reflection in the tri-framed mirror. My outfit consisted of a black V-neck Polo t-shirt with a pair of black Polo jeans and my all black Jordans. Checking myself in the mirror, I looked fly and the only thing that was missing was my black Rolex with the lizard skin band, my iced out black diamond bracelet with the matching chain, and earrings the size of dimes.

I looked like a tender and the women were going to be falling all over me. I started to text Izzy to see if I could meet up with her later, but I promised to back up off of her, so I'd chill for tonight. However, I was back at it tomorrow and a stop by her studio would be the first priority.

Pops and I had hit a few of his favorite spots and had some drinks with some of his friends, but for some reason, I kept thinking about Izzy. There was this one fine chick all on my tip, but I wasn't feeling her and was ready to go. She put her hand on Coltrane and asked if I wanted to get out of there and go somewhere more private. My boy didn't even move, so I knew it would be a waste of time. I excused myself from the table and went to the bathroom just to get away from her. Luckily Reece texted and asked if I wanted to meet her for a late dinner. I was over hanging with Pops and decided that meeting up with Reece was a good idea.

THE PLACE that Reece had me meet her at was packed. There was so many paparazzi outside that I figured someone famous must have been up in the restaurant. I pulled up to the valet hopping out like I was a celebrity. I handed the parking attendant my keys and proceeded inside of the restaurant.

The vibe was lit, and people were in there turned up. The bar was full of patrons and it looked like a private party was going on in the back. I hit Reece on the phone but saw a familiar face sitting at the bar. I wanted to go say hi to Izzy, but I decided to let her eat in peace. I remembered my conversation with Chess on our run, and he said it would be best if I let things happen organically. I told her that I had patience, but my body didn't seem to want to participate in the process because my dick always got hard whenever I saw her beautiful face.

"King!" someone called out as I walked to meet Reece. "King! Over here!" I turned to see who was calling me and to my surprise it was Jack. He walked up to me smiling coyly.

"What's up, Jack?"

"Hey, Kingdom. How are you tonight?"

"I'm chilling, and you can call me King." Jack smiled, glancing over his shoulder.

"Izzy's sitting over there at the bar," he said smiling.

"Oh yeah," I replied. "Tell her hello for me. I would come over to speak, but my sister's waiting for me."

"I see," Jack replied smugly. "I'll deliver the message and you have a good night."

"You do the same," I replied, walking away, but not before I surveyed the bar and saw Izzy sitting there talking with some guy. Her body looked sexy in the little black dress she was wearing. There wasn't much to it, but it covered all the right places. I especially liked the red Patent leather heels that she had on and... are her lips red? I could feel my dick hardening against my thigh. *Pull yourself together, King,* I told myself because I didn't want these women in here staring at my crotch instead of my face, so I thought about the time I caught my parents having sex in the kitchen and it instantly went down.

"King! There you are," Reece called out. "Over here!" I smiled, moving toward where she was sitting. There were a few other people at her table, and it was to my surprise because I thought it would only be us. "Little brother, I'm so glad you could join me."

"It looks like it's going to be more than just us tonight," I said smiling at her. She knew I didn't like being around people that I didn't know, but in true Reece fashion, she didn't give a fuck.

"King, I want you to meet a few friends of mine," Reece said, latching arms with me. She went around the table introducing me to everyone and I greeted all of them. "Sit down and I'll order you a drink."

"I'm ready to order some food, but I need to go do something first," I replied getting up out of my seat. "I'll be right back."

"Okay," she uttered as I walked away from the table headed to the bar. My attention was focused on Izzy until the bartender came down to help me.

"What can I get for you?" asked the bartender.

"I would like to order a cognac straight," I replied.

"Sure thing. Which brand would you like?" I told him the brand, and he disappeared down the bar. The way my body was positioned, Izzy couldn't see me while I stared at her lustfully waiting for my drink. When the bartender brought it back, I decided to order Izzy a drink, too.

"You see that sexy woman sitting down at the other end of the bar in that little black dress and the bright red hair? Can you send her a bottle of your best champagne and three glasses, please?" I requested. "How much is that with my drink?"

The bartender told me, and I reached into my pocket, pulling out a wad of cash. I pulled off a few hundred dollars passing it to him. I told him to keep the change and disappeared away from the bar. If that didn't leave a lasting impression on Izzy, then I don't know what to do. Maybe sending her a bunch of flowers and choco-lates would let her know that I'm serious about us getting together.

I went back over to the table with Reece and sat down next to her. My body was facing Izzy because I wanted to watch her from a distance. I saw when the bartender presented her with the bottle of champagne then looked down at the end of the bar for me. He had a stumped look on his face because I wasn't there, and Izzy flashed her million-dollar smile. I felt my boy thump against my leg, and a smile spread across my lips when she jumped from the cork being popped on the champagne. Izzy and her friends were cheering and dancing as the bartender poured their glasses.

"A penny for your thoughts, little brother. Where are you right now, King?" Reece whispered in my ear.

"Over there with that beautiful woman sitting at the end of the bar," I replied.

"Which one?" Reece questioned, looking up and down the bar.

"The brown-skinned one with those bright red lips and hair," I said lustfully.

"She must be something the way you said that," Reece teased. "You said that like you're lusting after her or something."

"I am," I replied frankly. "But she keeps saying that I'm too young."

"How old is she?" Reece asked curiously. "She looks like she's around your age. Maybe a little older like twenty-five or something." I looked at Reece, smirking.

"She's thirty-three," I replied.

"You're lying to me, King," Reece insisted. "She doesn't look like it."

"Well, she is," I replied smugly. "And get this… she's friends with Chess and Athlon. They went to college together."

"Get out of here!"

"Yep, big sis, and she was the one who styled Duchess's photo-shoot today. I'm very much attracted to her, but she keeps talking that 'I'm too old for you' shit and I think it's a cop-out."

"King, I think if you're really into her. You need to go over there and convince her to give you a shot," Reece suggested before taking a sip of her wine. "You only get one shot in this life, and you don't want it to be filled with a bunch of regrets."

Watching Izzy laugh and talk with her friends made me want to be over there with her so bad. I finished off my drink then put the glass on the table.

"I'm about to go over there and talk to her. I think you're right,

Reece, and I'm not going to listen to Chess and take his advice anymore." Reece laughed, kissing my cheek.

"Go get your woman, killer, and remember… you're the mutha-fuckin' man," Reece told me.

"I'm the muthafuckin' man," I replied in a low tone. I got up from the table and straightened my t-shirt out. I blew my breath into my hand, and the cognac smell damn near knocked me out. I reached into my pocket, pulled out a peppermint, and put it in my mouth as I made my way over to Izzy. She noticed me approaching her and a seductive smile came across her face.

"I guess I should thank you for sending me this bottle of cham-pagne," Izzy said, getting up off her stool. Her dress fell down and stopped just below her pussy, and I almost lost my fucking mind when I saw her bare camel toe.

"It was nothing," I replied, smiling back at her. "You did an exceptional job with my mother's photoshoot, and I sent over the bottle of champagne as a small gesture of thanks."

"Well thank you," she replied giggling and she wrapped her arms around my neck, hugging me tightly.

"You don't have on any panties," I whispered in her ear, rubbing my hand up the back of her thigh before wrapping my arm around her waist. Izzy pulled away slightly, not breaking eye contact with me as she held on to my neck. Her teeth bit down on her bottom lip, and it made me want to suck on it too.

"You're very observant, King," she replied. "And I see the woman that you're with is very observant as well because she's staring at us and I don't want to make her jealous."

"Let's make her jealous," I teased, staring into Izzy's eyes.

Next, I leaned down kissing her lips softly. We held it for a few seconds and Izzy didn't protest. I heard a few catcalls from Jack and that's when Izzy pulled away with her head held down in embar-rassment. She looked back up at me with a big smile on her face as her head went from side to side.

"You're a mess, King," Izzy said shyly, wiping my lips. I looked down at her thumb, but I didn't see any lipstick. "Don't worry. I didn't get any lipstick on you. There was a little slob on your lips from my wet mouth."

"I love your wet kisses, and I hope to get some more of them," I replied thirstily.

"Isn't your friend going to get mad at you?" Izzy questioned, looking over in Reece's direction. I turned my head to face her as well.

"Are you talking about that woman that's staring at us from across the room?" I asked curiously.

"Yes," she replied, staring back into my eyes.

"You don't have to worry about her. That's my big sister Reece, and she's the one who sent me over here."

"In that case pull up a stool," Izzy said grabbing my hand. She pulled me over to the bar and everyone shifted down to make room for me. I helped her back up on the stool and sat down beside her. She poured me a glass of champagne then jumped back into her conversation with her friends.

SEVENTEEN

Izzy

———————

KING WAS SITTING next to me and for some reason, I was relaxed. I wasn't anxious like I normally felt when he was around me, but I had been drinking. We had already drank several shots before King sent over the bottle of champagne.

"How are you feeling?" King whispered in my ear.

"I'm feeling good," I replied happily, leaning toward his ear. "I'd feel even better if you'd play with my pussy." King's eyes widened as he looked around the room. He peered down into my eyes while he studied my face intently.

"Are you sure you want me to do that?" King asked coyly.

"Did you hear my words? If not, let me rephrase myself. I want you to play in between my legs." Grabbing his hand, I put it under my dress. My legs spread open slightly, and his fingers brushed against my folds. "That's it, King. Fuck me with your fingers."

King's expression turned serious as he got up off the stool. He moved his body closer to mine, pushing two fingers inside of me. My chest was pressed against him and my head dropped on his shoulder as they went in and out of my wetness.

"Is this how you want it?" King asked lustfully in my ear.

"Yes..." my lips uttered breathlessly. "Make me feel good, baby."

King took his thumb, rubbing it repeatedly against my clit. My shallow breaths were blowing against his neck while my eyes surveyed the room. This boy was doing one hell of a job with his fingers, and his dick is probably even better.

"Let me hear you moan," King said before kissing my lips. Our tongues brushed against each other as I moaned against his lips. He pulled his fingers out of me, licking them hungrily before putting them back inside of my goodness. "Gosh... you're so wet, Izzy." And there was nothing I could say to that.

"Uuuhhhhh," came out of my mouth, and it got the attention of Jack.

"Your boy's watching us," King informed me, staring deeply into my eyes. "Maybe we should give him a show."

"It's all on you... What you wanna do?"

"Hhhhmmmm... You're a real freak, Miss James," King purred as he quickened his pace.

"Uuuhhh... huh..." managed to come out of my mouth because my orgasm was about to hit. My head dropped back down onto King's shoulder once more as my body humped his fingers. The grip my arms had on his neck tightened, and my hips lifted up off the stool slightly.

King must have felt my walls contract because there was a silly grin draped on his lips. His thumb kept strumming, and his fingers kept pushing while my hips kept pumping as my orgasm hit.

"Mmmmmm..." was the only sound that came out as my teeth bit down on my bottom lip. My forehead was buried in the nape of his neck as the moans were continuing to come. My core was tingling, and my entire body felt my release.

"Cum for me, Izzy," King whispered in my ear. "You look so fucking sexy right now."

"Ssshhhh..." was all I could muster because my knees were slightly shaking uncontrollably.

"You two look like you're having fun down there," Jack said smugly.

"We are," King replied, putting his fingers in his mouth, licking all of my juices off them then kissed my lips sensually.

"Did I miss something?" Jack asked looking around confused.

"You didn't miss nothing, baby," I replied curtly. "Now, carry on and worry about Jose while I handle this situation down here."

KING WAS STARING at me lustfully when I got back from the bathroom. My legs were wet from that good fingering that occurred, and I had to freshen that situation up. I was absolutely starving when I got back to the table and the waiter had brought over our food.

"That looks good," King said staring at my food. "Can you ask the bartender for a menu so I can order something for myself."

"You can share with me. This is a lot of food, and I'm not going to eat all of it. Do you like your steak well done because that's how this Porterhouse was prepared," I explained.

"I like my meat cooked all the way through, too," King replied. "The only pink meat I like to eat is pussy, and I'm very selective about that." A huge smile spread across my face as I placed a fork full of potatoes in my mouth.

"You want to share a fork?" I asked before licking the back of it.

"I want to share those red ass lips," he replied, kissing me softly. He licked my top one as we pulled away, and I felt my center heat up again. Leaning into King my lips migrated to his ear.

"Booooyyyy... you better stop playing before I fuck you right here at the bar," I moaned.

"What are you waiting on?" he asked, pulling away from me so I could see the seriousness in his expression. "I've already played with your pussy right here, so we might as well finish." We both smiled at each other because the sexual tension had gotten stronger.

"I'm going to need for the two of you to cut it out," Jack declared. "There is too much PDA going on at this bar between the two of you, and I'm afraid y'all are going to break out fucking right here in front of us.

"Leave them alone," Jose said pushing Jack on the arm. "I'm

getting turned on just watching them." I looked over at them and blushed because I was really feeling myself.

"I'm King, and who are you?"

"I'm sorry, King. How rude of me. This is Jack's fiancé Jose. Jose, this is King," I explained. Jose looked at me strangely for a second, but then he realized who I was talking about.

"This is Kingdom, right?" Jose said, smiling at us coyly. "I've heard so much about you, but they didn't fully explain how gorgeous you are." King laughed, but I could tell he felt a bit uncomfortable.

"Don't worry, King," Jack said wrapping his arm around Jose's neck. "We know you're not trading, and our Miss Elizabeth James is smitten by you."

"I'm smitten by Miss James as well, and I don't know why she keeps shooting me down whenever I proposition her to let me show her a good time," King replied boldly.

I put a forkful of baked potato up to his face and bit my bottom lip as I watched him take the food into his mouth. He chewed it slowly while staring at me intently and our eyes never left each other's.

"You want to get out of here?" I asked softly.

"Yes," King replied abruptly. "My car is valeted. Did you drive?"

"No. I rode here with Jack and Jose."

"Can we settle up her tab?" King yelled out holding up his hand. The bartender looked at him and waved his hand to let King know that he'd heard him.

"Where are the two of you going?" Jack asked nosily.

"We're about to go fuck because we've got some unfinished business," I said, and King was definitely in agreement.

EIGHTEEN

Izzy

_____

Izzy

We were on our way out of the restaurant when the woman that was staring approached us. She was looking me up and down and at first, I got offended. How is this bitch going to come check me over, and I hope I don't have to kick off my shoes and beat a bitch ass over some dick, because she can have his ass!

"Izzy, I want you to meet my big sister Reece. We have the same father but different mothers," King explained.

"It's nice to meet you," Reece said, extending her hand.

"Hello," I replied pleasantly as we shook hands.

"Normally, King keeps his female friends to himself, so you must be special if he's introducing you to me," Reece said smugly.

"It's nothing like that. We're just about to go have sex." I replied, smiling. My liquor was in full swing, and there's no telling what else would come out of my mouth.

King cleared his throat as he looked at me in disbelief. A low chuckle came out of his mouth, and he squeezed my hand, but his sister didn't see the humor in it at all.

"I see," she replied. "King, you've got a live one here. Don't forget to strap up."

"I won't," King replied. "I love you, sissy, and I'll call you tomorrow."

"You better," she replied. "Izzy it was a pleasure to meet you."

"The pleasure was all mine," I said, giggling uncontrollably. "And I'm sorry for being so crass."

"You sound like you've had a lot to drink, so I completely understand," Reece replied graciously. "Have a good night you two, and be safe."

———

KING PULLED up in front of a security gate pressing the code into the keypad. The large wrought iron gate opened up and King slowly pulled his car into the driveway. We were up in the hills near the Hollywood sign and the lavish house that sat in front of us impressed me.

King pulled up in front of the garage and put his car in park. He put his hand on my thigh and leaned over to kiss my lips, but I put my hand against them smiling. He grabbed my wrist, pulling it away then smashed his lips against mine forcefully. Opening my mouth, I welcomed his tongue while we kissed nastily. He slid his hand up my dress brushing his fingers against my wetness. Pulling away from me, King stared lustfully into my eyes.

"I need to hurry up and get you into the house before I fuck you in my car," King said, opening his door.

"Would that be a bad thing? I mean ain't nothing wrong with a little front seat action."

King looked at me and laughed before he exited the car. He walked around to my side opening the door and offering me his hand, which I took gladly. He helped me out of the car and I leaned against it while he shut the door.

"You must really want this pussy," I teased. "I mean you kept pressing your big ass dick against my ass every time you saw me."

"Don't act like you don't want this dick, Izzy. I saw you drooling over it every time we were in the same room together. You know you wanted to suck it when you had this muthafucka in your hand."

"Touché again, young man," I replied giggling. "However, you might fuck me like a little boy." King looked at me like he was very offended.

"After I serve you this dick, my age isn't going to be a problem anymore," King assured me. He grabbed me by the hand and led me to the front door. He pressed a code into the keypad, and one of the grand steel doors opened. "After you," he said ushering me inside. He walked over to another keypad located near the door and pressed a few numbers. He turned back around and directed all of his attention to me.

I wasn't that far away from him when I slid the straps of my dress down over my shoulders. I let it fall down from my body to the floor then stepped out of it as I walked further into the house. Turning around to face King, who was staring at me hungrily, I ran my hand through my hair and slid it down my neck slowly. Next, they went down to my breast and my fingers grazed across my nipple and from there they continued journeying down my stomach until my fingers went across my hairless pussy. I stopped in between my legs, playing with my clit suggestively.

"Where is your room? I'm so wet," I said, wrapping my free arm over my head. A giggle escaped my lips like a schoolgirl, and King rushed over to me urgently. He cupped my face in both of his hands and thrust his tongue inside of my mouth. We tongued each other down for a few minutes before King picked me up and threw me over his shoulder.

"Oh my God, you're strong!" I shouted, laughing.

"You ain't felt strength yet," he replied, walking toward some steps. "I'm about to fuck the shit out of you in those bad ass shoes."

King walked into a dark bedroom, placing me down on my feet. He grabbed the bottom of his t-shirt pulling it over his head. I grabbed his belt and undid it eagerly. My fingers popped his button out of the eyelid before they went down inside of his underwear. His dick was already hard against my hand, and I wrapped my fingers around the shaft moving them vigorously up and down as my lips planted soft kisses against his chest.

"Not tonight," he said, pulling my hand out of his pants. "I'm going to drive my dick so far up in your pussy that you're going to feel it in your chest."

"You promise?" I asked enthusiastically, biting down on my lip.

"I promise," King assured me, stepping out of his shoes. He pulled his pants down to his ankles and his dick fell out hitting me on the stomach. I sat down on the bed ready to be taken as my legs parted and my fingers played with coochie.

King stepped out of his pants as he walked toward me with urgency. The force of his body made me back up on the bed, but my legs were wide open and ready to receive him. All ten inches of that dick was going to be felt up inside of my womb and I hoped he knocked my back out so that I'd have an excuse not to go to work tomorrow.

King leaned over me and kissed my lips softly while he spread my legs wider with his body. He rubbed his erection against my folds and pushed deep inside of me as I gasped at the pressure then exhaled slowly.

"Can you take all of this dick?" King asked playfully pushing deep up in me.

"Does a fat kid love cake?" I replied sarcastically, and he pushed all of his girth inside of me, again. "Aaaahhhhh," I uttered as my walls were being stretched out. He pulled back half way then pushed all of himself inside of me again as my back arched. This shit felt wonderful, and I couldn't wait for him to really serve me the dick and that came faster than expected.

King humped inside of me like a little jackrabbit, and I must admit that it felt quite uncomfortable after a minute. It was like he purposefully was pounding my walls, and I couldn't understand why he was doing it because we hadn't built up to it yet. It was understandable if he was doing it pleasurably, but it felt like he didn't know what he was doing, and no one took the time to show him correctly.

"Owww!" I shouted, and he looked down at me, smiling.

"You like this dick I'm serving you?" he uttered arrogantly.

"No, I don't," I replied smugly, and he looked at me confused.

"What? You're not enjoying this?" he asked, looking dumb-founded, then he stopped.

"I'm sorry King, but I'm not enjoying this experience. I don't know who you're used to fucking, but I don't like unnecessary rough sex. I could understand if you were punishing me for something that I did wrong, but that's not the case, and I don't like it." I pushed him up off of me, and he fell on his back. I rolled over on top of him because it was time to take charge.

"I don't understand," said King, sounding confused. "I was straight dicking you down."

"I know, baby, but it was not in a good way. You're fucking me like you've paid for the pussy, and I want you to fuck me like you want the pussy," I replied before leaning down and kissing his lips softly.

I reached down in between my legs, grabbed his dick, and started rubbing it against my folds before it slid deep inside of me. I held my head back and moaned as his dick hit the curve of my fallopian tubes. It had been a long time since I had that happen. Lifting myself up, I stopped halfway then slid back down, rocking my hips in a front to back motion. I tightened my muscles around his dick, and his eyes widened freakishly.

"Do that again," he said and bit his bottom lip.

I obliged him as my goodness moved up and down his rod. I placed my hand on his stomach and continued to ride his dick slowly. King was biting his bottom lip and playing with my nipples, which made this feel even better. A man that could multitask was all right in my book, especially if they know what they're doing. That's why my pace sped up when I felt myself about to orgasm.

Leaning down, I kissed his lips passionately as he stroked my clit with his fingers. He lifted up his head and latched onto my nipple. He sucked his jaws tightly while his tongue flickered back and forth against my nub. My orgasm erupted through my body as I called out in ecstasy. His dick felt so good as I came on it. My body fell forward, and King caught my nipple into his mouth and bit down on it causing my orgasm to go into overdrive.

"You like this dick don't you," King said humping up inside of me.

"I'm going to love this dick once I teach you how to fuck me," I replied before kissing his lips. He continued to hump up inside of me until another orgasm hit.

I leaned over him and let my nipple brush his lips. He took it greedily into his mouth and sucked on it as if he were nursing. I screamed out in triumph as my body tingled and shook uncontrollably. My pace slowed down because he still had to nut, and I didn't want to be selfish since King was so generous.

Tightening my muscles around his erection once more King gripped my hips as my body rocked back and forth. He was about to nut, so he slid himself out of me. I took his dick in my hand and moved it vigorously until he erupted all over it.

"Fuuuuuuck! You are amazing, Izzy." King howled as his warm essences ran all over my hand. He kissed my lips passionately before I pulled away smiling at him wickedly.

"I ended up fucking the shit out of you, but maybe next time you can return the favor." I got up off of the bed and headed toward the bathroom. King decided to join me, and we took a sensual shower where I made him nut once more with my magical hand. There was something about King that made my nature rise, and it just might be a little harder not to walk away after tonight.

NINETEEN

King

I WAS LYING on my stomach when I woke up out of my sleep. I reached over to feel Izzy's soft sexy body next to mine, but the only thing I felt was the mattress. Jumping up, my eyes stared around the room for a second and they landed on her red heels over on the floor, so I knew she hadn't left. That was a relief, but I had to check myself for a minute. Usually, I don't give a fuck about a chick leaving without waking me up, but for some strange reason, I felt differently this morning. Last night was dope, and never in my entire life have I had a woman take charge in bed like she did last night. I couldn't believe she said she wasn't enjoying all of this dick, but she came several times though.

I got up out of the bed and stretched as I walked to the bathroom. There were towels all over the floor, but that was from the shower that we had taken last night. She made me nut back to back by jacking me off then sexing me again. Izzy was a beast and I'm trying to get up in them guts again this morning.

I flushed the toilet after relieving myself and went over to the sink. I washed my hands first then cleaned my face. I brushed my teeth and rinsed my mouth out with Listerine before flashing my winning smile at myself in the mirror.

I headed downstairs and smelled breakfast cooking in the air. A smile came across my face because my soon to be bae had cooked for me. How special is that? I made it to the bottom of the steps, rounded them into the living room and headed straight back into the kitchen. Pops was standing at the stove flipping pancakes, and Izzy was sitting on one of the barstools. They were in the middle of a conversation as I walked further into the room and stood in the middle of the floor. Pops turned around and noticed me with a big smile on his face.

"Good morning, sleepy head. I guess somebody got worn out last night," Pops joked while Izzy looked back at me, smiling.

"Good morning, King," Izzy said warmly. I noticed she had on the top to the pajama pants I was wearing and a smile spread across my face.

"Good morning beautiful," I said as I walked up on her kissing her lips softly and letting it linger for a second. My grandfather watched us before he turned back around to tend to the skillets on the stove. "Did you sleep well?" I asked, sitting down next to Izzy.

"I slept like a baby," she replied coyly. "Your bed is amazing, and your mattress is so comfortable. However, why didn't you tell me that you stayed with Sam? I was under the impression that you lived by yourself. Well no, I thought you lived with your parents."

"I have a room there, but I don't live there. My mother thinks that I live in my apartment on campus, but I lied to her. If she knew that I stayed in this house, she would be over here damn near every day."

"And we don't want that to happen," Pops added, placing a plate of food in front of Izzy.

"Are you hungry, King?" Pops asked.

"I'm famished," I replied and winked at Izzy. She blushed and lifted her eyebrows up at me.

"I wonder why you're so hungry," she said playfully.

"It could have something to do with what you did to me last night," I replied. Pops put a plate down in front of me as I stared at Izzy feeling horny. "Thanks, Pops," I said picking up one of the sausages. The plate had four pancakes, eggs with cheese, grits and three turkey sausage patties on it.

"You're welcome, grandson," he replied. "You need to eat to refuel your energy." Izzy looked over at me and giggled.

"This guy has youth on his side," Izzy said wittingly. "I'm the one who needs to refuel if I'm going to keep up with him."

"Oh… you can keep up with me," I teased, and Izzy's cheeks turned red. She looked over at Pops, and he returned her gaze, but I didn't like the way they were staring at one another. Izzy's phone went off, and she stared down at it. A frown came across her face and she picked it up off the counter.

"Excuse me for a second," Izzy said and got up off the stool.

"Okay," I replied as she walked out of the room. I noticed how cute she looked in my pajama top, but I wanted to see her naked again. My Pops was watching her as well, and I turned to face him because I wanted to know what that was about. "Why are you watching Izzy like that… and what was that look the two of you gave each other a minute ago before she got that call?"

"What?" Pops asked, staring at me questionably. "I just wanted to make sure that Izzy was out of earshot before I congratulated you on your conquest." Pops looked past me and down the hallway into the living room. "How was it, son?"

"It was good, Pops," I replied. "I mean it was better than good. It was great!" I looked behind me to see if Izzy heard me because that came out loudly. "I mean, she took control and rocked my world." A smile appeared on my grandfather's face and he took a sip from his cup.

"I told you, King, that she's seasoned. That's a grown woman that you're dealing with and not one of those young girls you're used to fucking."

"I don't just fuck young girls," I replied aggressively. "I've fucked women older than Izzy."

"I know, King, because I'm the one who hooked you up with them," Pops replied smugly. "I'm just giving you some advice so the next time you have sex with her. She doesn't have to take control."

"Why did you say that? Did she say something to you?" I asked, staring at him questionably.

"You just said out of your own mouth that she took over," Pops replied and took a drink from his cup. "But now that you mentioned it, she did make a comment about your sex and don't go getting an attitude with her."

"What the fuck is she doing discussing what we did last night with you?" I snapped. "Why couldn't she say something to me about it?"

"Because she probably thought that you would blow up on her like you just did me," Pops replied. "Calm down and eat your food, King. We'll talk more about it later." I sat there stewing because I couldn't believe that Izzy said something to my grandfather about my sex game that she couldn't say to my face. I gets plenty of pussy, and her pussy wasn't the only thang popping in the city. I had a straight attitude and wanted to know why she didn't talk to me.

Izzy walked back into the kitchen fully dressed with those heels I loved on and her purse in hand. She strolled up to me with a sad look on her face, and I wondered if she overheard our conversation. I was pissed at her, but I didn't want her to leave. We had some stuff to talk about and my sex game was one of them.

"I'm sorry, King, but I really have to go. My client just called me, and she needs me to help her get ready for an unexpected appearance," Izzy explained.

"Let me put some clothes on so that I can drop you off," I replied getting up from the chair.

"That won't be necessary. I called an Uber to come get me," Izzy explained. "But you can walk me to the door." She smiled warmly at me, and my temper went down a few notches. She was beautiful with no makeup, and I couldn't resist her big slanted eyes.

"I can walk you to the door," I replied dryly.

"Thanks for breakfast, Sam, and it was good to see you," Izzy said waving at Pops.

"The pleasure was all mine," Pops replied and held up his coffee cup. Izzy grabbed my hand and intertwined her fingers into mine.

We walked to the door in silence, then she turned to face me when we made it to the entrance.

"Please don't be mad at me, King," Izzy said walking closer to me. "I overheard some of the conversation that you were having with your grandfather, and I should apologize to you for going behind your back and saying something to Sam instead of addressing it with you. I guess I'm a little bit out of practice with the rules of engagement, but I go way back with your grandfather, and we've always talked openly."

"It sounds like you should be fucking him instead of me then," I shot back. Izzy looked at me, and I could tell she was offended. Her phone buzzed, and she looked down at it.

"My Uber's here, King," she said softly. She placed her hand on my cheek and planted a kiss in the middle of my forehead. She pulled away staring at me for a second. "Bye, King," she said softly. Then she opened the door and left. I just stood there staring as it closed behind her with my head held down with my chin resting on my chest. This was not how things were supposed to go. We should have been headed upstairs to work things out. This shit can't be happening.

TWO WEEKS Later

The weekend had finally made it, and a brother was looking forward to getting into some trouble. It was Halloween night, and I needed to get out and have some fun. It'd been two weeks since that awkward morning with Izzy and Pops. I hadn't talked to either of them since that day. I'd been staying at my apartment on campus, and it actually isn't that bad. I'd been fucking co-eds of all nationalities and I even hooked up with Sarah again for old times sake. There's nothing wrong with my sex game. Izzy and Pops got me fucked up!

My boy Harrison convinced me to join him and a couple of our friends for a night out of drinking and bad decisions. We all chose to be comic book heroes and naturally, Batman and Superman were the first ones to go. I chose to be Black Panther because all my

Nubian women were going crazy for the African prince, and I wanted them to throw that ass in my direction. What can I say? I'm the nigga that Gucci's singing about in his song. *"a dog, I'm a dog, I'm a dog, I'm a dog!"* and all the ladies love it... all ten inches of it!"

We decided to go on Hollywood Boulevard because that's where all the freaks were going to be. I grabbed my old school 1967 kissing door Lincoln Continental out of storage to floss. A superhero always pushed a fly ass ride, and since my superhero drove spaceships and I don't got that shit, I was going to drive vintage because all the hoes love an old school car.

Harrison said that he heard about a dope ass Halloween party that was going on at one of the clubs on Hollywood Boulevard. We pulled up at the spot and parked valet. Harrison rode with me and our other three boys Que, Justin and Laron were in Que's Camaro. I'm sure you can guess what superhero he was for the night. We all had on t-shirts with their symbol on them, but this nigga Que had on a black cape, and Harrison had on a red one because he was Superman. Chelsea found me a beaded bracelet that looked like the one Black Panther wore in the movie. I fucked her real good in my parent's bed the next day after Izzy dissed me and she sucked me off the other day in the library on a dare. I was just in 'don't give a fuck mode' that's all.

The energy was electrifying as we made our way through the club. Bitches were out butt ass naked, and titties were hanging everywhere. We made our way over to the bar, but not without making a few stops to flirt with the ladies. We had smoked a loud blunt on the ride over to the club. Que had some Ecstasy, so we popped a pill earlier while we drank a bottle before we left the apartment. I felt good as a muthafucka, and some man's daughter was going to be my victim for the night... I meant my damsel in distress.

I placed our drink orders and waited for the bartender to bring it to us. I turned to check out the crowd, and that's when I saw this sexy woman dressed in some type of bodysuit. I don't know what type of material it was made out of, but I could see all of her ass crack when her rainbow-colored hair swayed from side to side.

"Check that chick out right there in that bodysuit with the rainbow hair," I told Harrison.

"Her hair is not really rainbow," Laron replied. "It's blue, turquoise, purple, and fuchsia. That's not rainbow." I stared at that boy in disbelief because I couldn't believe this grown ass man just said that shit to me.

"Who the fuck cares Laron?" I replied smugly. "That bitch with the colorful hair is bad, and I'm about to push up on her."

I walked off from the bar, and I could hear my boys cheering me on. I pulled a peppermint out of my pocket and popped it in my mouth. I tugged at the bottom of my t-shirt to make sure it was fitting right. I stepped up to the misses with my winning smile on my face and tapped her lightly on the shoulder.

"Excuse me, but I couldn't help but to notice how dope you look in your costume," I said standing closely behind her. "Can you tell me what your are?" The woman turned around and I found myself face to face with Izzy.

TWENTY

Izzy

———————

THE HAIRS on the back of my neck stood up because I would recognize that voice from anywhere. I took a deep breath before I turned around and there stood Kingdom McDaniel live and in the flesh. I looked at him smugly and put my mask up against my face.

"I'm a fairy, and it was nice seeing you again." I turned back around and went to walk away, but I felt his hand grab my arm. He pulled me back to him and I fell against his body. "Let me go, King. Don't be manhandling me," I protested.

"Calm your ass down, Izzy," he replied sternly. "I should be the one with the attitude, not you." I looked up into his gorgeous green eyes and my heart fluttered. His dreads were crinkly and hanging down over his shoulders. He had on a solid black t-shirt with the Black Panther necklace on it. My eyes gazed over the rest of him and he had on a pair of black jeans and some black Cole Haan leather tennis shoes. King always looked so sexy in his clothes, and I so wanted to peel his ass out of them and fuck him on the floor.

"Why didn't you return my calls?" I asked with an attitude.

"Why did you tell my Pops that my sex game was wack?" he countered.

"What?" I shouted. "I never said that!"

"Are you sure, because he said he had to talk to me about my sex game, and something about how I shouldn't have let you take over in bed," King retorted. "Did you tell my grandfather that I didn't know how to fuck, because that's some bullshit?"

People around us were staring, and a few of them started laughing. King looked around and glared at all of them and their nosy asses either walked away or turned their heads.

"No, King. I didn't tell your grandfather that," I replied, feeling frustrated. I leaned in and whispered into King's ear. "What I told him is that you have a big dick, but you don't know how to control it."

"That's saying that I don't know how to fuck," King countered. "Look, I get plenty of pussy, and the only thing that bitches tell me is that their pussies hurt afterward because I beat that shit up."

"Exactly King, and you're not going to hurt my pussy," I replied turning my lips up at him. "I enjoyed riding your dick and would have loved to do it again and again, but you dissed me, and I'm cool on you." He stared at me with a frustrated look on his face.

"I thought women liked getting their pussy beat up," King said, staring into my eyes.

"We do, but sex shouldn't be painful, and it was very uncomfortable when you were pounding my walls like that," I explained. "I'm a grown woman, and I know how to open up my mouth and tell you how I want to be fucked. Now, I don't know why Sam said what he did to you, and again, I apologize for even saying anything to him because that was wrong. The only thing that I wish could have happened was that you would have given me a chance to explain myself instead of ignoring my phone calls." King stared into my eyes, and my core began to tingle.

"There you are, birthday girl!" Jack shouted. "Let's go over to the other side because the gang has shots lined up for you." He looked over at King and did a double take. "Why, Kingdom... how the hell are you?" King stared into my eyes with a hint of contempt.

"Why didn't you tell me that today was your birthday?" King asked sternly.

"Because that's not what you wanted to hear," I replied frankly. "It was good seeing you, King. Take care of yourself."

I leaned in and kissed his lips then grabbed Jack's hand and walked away leaving King standing there. He watched as the crowd swallowed us up. A bit of sadness came over me, but this situation was water under the bridge. It was my birthday, and I wasn't going to let Kingdom McDaniel ruin it. He hurt my feelings two weeks ago and made me feel like I was a jump off to him. I apologized for running my mouth, but if he wanted to act like a child about the situation, then I was going to let him.

———

JACK FED me several shots to help me get over the uncomfortable encounter I had with King. We went out on the balcony and smoked a few joints and my anxiety miraculously disappeared. I was fucked up and felt good about it because it was my muthafuckin' birthday. Drake's song "God's Plan" came on, and I damn near lost my mind because that's my song. I shouted the words to the song at the top of my lungs while Jack danced up on me. We heard a bunch of whistles blowing, and the bottle service girls were walking in our direction with the sprinklers crackling everywhere. Jack and I moved out of the way so that they could get by, but the first girl stopped in front of me and the other three girls stopped next to her. They were each holding bottles, and King, along with some other guys, that were dressed like superheroes came walking up too.

King came over and stood in front of me for a few seconds staring me down, intensely. He grabbed my hand and pulled me to him then kissed my lips tenderly. People around us cheered, and the bottle service girls blew their whistles.

"Happy birthday, Elizabeth James," King cooed, staring deeply into my eyes.

"Thank you," I replied and kissed his lips again. We held our kiss for a few more seconds then we pulled away from each other.

"What is this you have on your body, and why are you showing people my shit?" King questioned. I lifted an eyebrow at him.

"How you figure this is your shit?" I asked, staring at him like he was crazy. "It's been two weeks since I've heard from your raggedy ass, and now you're going to try to come lay claim on all of this?"

"Shut the fuck up, and give me a kiss," King demanded. He brought his lips within a breath of mine and stared into my eyes while he held my arm firmly. My nipples got hard, and it was obvious to everyone who was staring at me. I tilted my head up so that our lips met, and he pressed his against mine firmly. I melted into his arms and forgot about having an attitude. I was going to enjoy my birthday with King because this was so unexpected.

King and I were dancing on one another when he held his hands over my head.

"Open your mouth," he said, and I looked up at his hand.

"What is that?" I asked frowning.

"Do you trust me?" he asked. I looked at him questionably with a frown still on my face. "It's an x-pill. Do you take ecstasy?"

"I do, but I don't let men randomly put pills into my mouth," I explained.

"I'm not some random dude, and eventually, you're going to be my gal," he replied. "Now, open your mouth."

I did what he asked, and he put the pill into my mouth. I took a sip from my cup and he kissed me on my temple. We continued to dance, and after about fifteen minutes, I felt even more amazing. I no longer felt as drunk and all I wanted to do was dance.

"What is this shit on your body?" King asked again, rubbing my ass.

"It's latex. I'm a walking condom!" We both laughed, and Jack joined in because he heard what I said.

"I painted it on her and it took a long time," Jack explained. "We had to make sure it was evenly spread, and her kitty did not want to cooperate."

"Don't tell King that," I said and hit Jack on the arm. "Don't listen to him, baby. He shouldn't be telling you my secrets."

"I haven't told him shit yet," Jack replied. "Did I mention how you cried a few days ago because he hadn't returned your calls?" I looked at Jack then over at King with a mortified look on my face.

I'm a thirty-four-year-old woman, and there was no way I should have been crying over this little boy, but I hadn't orgasmed like I did with him in a long ass time. I figured I could teach him how to fuck me like I liked, and we could both be happy and satisfied.

"I made you cry, Izzy?" King asked sincerely. He lifted my chin and kissed me on the lips. "I'm sorry, baby, and I promise I'm going to make it up to you tonight when I take you home."

"You're taking me home?" I replied, smiling.

"Not if you don't want me to," he said in an understanding tone.

"I want you to," I said and kissed his lips urgently. I tried to pull away, but he grabbed me by my hair. He slid his tongue into my mouth, and I welcomed it greedily. We tongue kissed nastily, and I didn't give a fuck that we were out in public because this fine young tender was all on the t-i-p of my dick!

TWO HOURS LATER

"I'm ready to go," King whispered into my ear. "Are you ready?" I was fucked up and kept on giggling while the music willed my body. The x-pill had taken over me, and I felt like dancing the night away.

"What are we going to go do?" I asked grinding up against him.

"We're about to go to your house and screw," King replied.

"Are you going to do it like I like?" I asked him playfully.

"I'm going to fuck you real good, Izzy. I promise you, baby," he replied. My back was to him, and he reached around my body cupping my camel toe. He played in between my legs as my body continued to grind against him.

"I need to tell Jack that I'm leaving. I'll be right back," I informed him.

"Hurry up, Izzy. My dick is hard, and I'm ready to be inside of you."

"King... your mouth is so nasty."

"You like it," he shot back and all I could do is smile at him, walking away to go find Jack.

Jack was over by the bar grinding up against Jose. I told him that I was leaving with King, and he stared at me with an attitude, so that meant he was about to fuss at me. It was a lecture that was definitely not needed.

"Are you sure you want to leave with him?" Jack asked with a bit of an attitude. "We were supposed to be celebrating your birthday, and King somehow bombarded into our thing and interrupted our plans." I gathered Jack into my arms and hugged him tightly.

"I love you, Jack, and thank you for a wonderful birthday. You spoiled me today by taking me for a spa day and then dinner at my favorite restaurant. You are the best friend in the whole wide world, and I'm forever grateful to have you in my life!" I hugged him tightly again, and I felt my shoulder getting wet. I pulled away and saw Jack tearing, so I really knew it was time for all of us to leave.

"I love you so much, Izzy, and I don't want to see you get hurt or disappointed again," he sobbed. "I know I'm a drunk mess right now, but bitch, it's your muthafuckin' birthday, and we got turnt for your day!"

"Yes, we did," I replied. "I'll call you in the morning."

"You better not, bitch, because I'm not going to answer," Jack said and turned up his lips. We both laughed and shared a kiss on cheek then I turned and walked away. It was time to fight through this crowd to go find King so that he could take me home and knock this coochie down for the one time.

TWENTY-ONE

King

___

I WAS WAITING for Izzy to walk back up when Harrison came rushing over to me. He was sweating profusely, and his jaw was moving a mile a minute. Those pills he took had him wired for sound, so my friend was definitely on one.

"Aye, King, let's go," Harrison said walking up on me. "We got a group of chicks over on the other side and they want to go chill with us."

"That sounds cool, but I'm about to leave with Izzy," I replied looking for her. "It's her birthday, and I'm about to give her some birthday dick!"

"Ain't she the chick who told your grandfather that your sex game was wack?" Harrison asked with an attitude. "Man, if I were you, I wouldn't want to fuck that bitch again."

"You need to watch your mouth and besides, you're not me. It was a misunderstanding all the way around, and Pops made this into something that could have been avoided. Come to think of it, I need to go talk to him tomorrow."

"C'mon, King, let's go fuck the Amazons. They're dressed like the bitches from Wonder Woman, and it's our duty to go knock those thots down," Harrison insisted.

"I hear you, Harrison, but you're not hearing me," I replied a little more forcefully. "I'm about to take Izzy home and fuck the shit out of her. I'm not going to repeat myself again, so catch a ride with Que, and I'll holler at you tomorrow."

Harrison looked at me with disappointment on his face. We had been kicking it hard for the past two weeks, and I was sure he's pissed because I was picking a broad over hanging with the fellas.

"All right, bruh," Harrison replied. "I hope your dick can't get hard."

"Now, that would be tragic," said Izzy, walking up on us. "But I got magical powers that can make that big muthafucka rise." She rubbed her hand against my dick, and it lifted up into it. "See! I made that muthafucka thump." Izzy and I laughed, but Harrison stared at us not amused.

"You do have magical powers," fell from my lips, and we kissed each other tenderly.

"Have fun," Harrison said dryly before walking away.

"What's his problem?" Izzy asked, frowning.

"Don't worry about Harrison," I replied, chuckling. "He's just mad because I won't go with him to fuck the Amazons."

"The Amazons?" Izzy questioned. She looked at me strangely then realized what I was talking about. "They don't want to go with those Amazons. They're actually a bunch of trannies dressed up like the ones from Wonder Woman. You better go tell your friends before they get the surprise of their life."

"Fuck them niggas," I replied frankly. "They should know the difference between a woman and a man. Besides, Harrison was giving me shit about leaving with you."

"He did?" Izzy replied with a frown on her face. "Why? I didn't do anything to him."

"I already told you, Izzy, but that nigga ain't important. The only thing you need to worry about is me redeeming myself because I'm about to give you the fuck of your life." Izzy placed her hand against her chest and batted her eyes at me.

"Why, King… I never heard such charming words in my life," she replied in a southern accent. We laughed as we made our way to the door, and my eyes scoped the crowd for Harrison to give him a heads up about his new female friends. However, he wasn't anywhere in sight, and a nigga wasn't about to go looking for him.

We got into my car, and Izzy went crazy over it. She talked about how much she loved old school cars because they have roomy front and back seats. Her body was leaning against mine, and her hand ventured down into my lap.

"What are you doing?"

"Just looking for something," Izzy replied unfastening my belt then my button. "The only thing you need to do is focus on the road."

Izzy leaned down and took the head of my dick inside of her mouth, and it completely threw me off. I sucked in some air and blew it out slowly as her mouth engulfed over half of my joint. Coltrane stiffened and spread Izzy's jaws, but it didn't stop her from going to work. The way her tongue went up and down my dick and the slurping noises she was making was driving me wild. My leg was shaking uncontrollably, and the car almost veered off the road.

Izzy came up off of it and spit on the head while her hand continued to move up and down and her tongue circled her lips. The soft moan her throat was making was driving a brother crazy.

"Did you like that, King?"

"I loved that shit. Why did you stop?"

"Well, you almost killed us, so it might be best if we save it until we're at my house," Izzy explained. "It would be messed up if the headline read 'Celebrity Stylist, Izzy James, Dies in a Car Crash while Sucking a Dick'."

"That does sound fucked up, but I promise, baby, we're not going to crash," was my counter-argument. Izzy looked at me smiling then went back to work on Coltrane.

Izzy's mouth felt excellent on my joint as her jaw muscles worked the girth. Her lips tightened around my shaft and she occasionally deep throated it causing her to gag. Dragging her tongue up to the head of my dick, she sucked it hard and fast while her hand moved rapidly stroking it. This cap that she was giving me was amazing, and my body stiffened when the moment of truth arrived.

My hips move in a circular motion as my dick stiffened against her tongue. The warm thick nut came shooting out into her mouth and Izzy gobbled it up like a champ. She licked the sides of it stroking me relentlessly and continued to deep throat all of me.

"Damn, Izzy! You're a beast with your head game," I moaned as she continued to hungrily suck me off. We were almost at her house, but it didn't look like we were going to make it.

Izzy rose up and looked at me seductively as she wiped the corners of her mouth. Next, without any warning, she climbed on my lap and once again the car swerved over to the side. Izzy wrapped her arms around my neck while my eyes tried to stay focused on the road. Her silly giggle made me smile while we continued down the street.

"Your ass is going to get us killed out here," I fussed, looking over her shoulder.

"I'm horny and all worked up. We're almost at my house, but I don't know if my body can wait much longer," Izzy moaned in my ear.

"Hold on, lil' mama, because it's going to be on as soon as we get into your house."

Izzy was quite vulnerable and forthcoming with her feelings as she whispered her thoughts and feelings into my ear. The car automatically parked itself because we were kissing and feeling all over each other the rest of the car ride and by the time we got out of the car, both of us were ready for round two, and on my mama, I was going to lay it down on her ass like a porn star.

"Welcome to my home," Izzy said inviting me inside. She shut the door behind me and secured the locks. She walked up behind me, wrapping her arms around my waist. I felt her hands working rapidly unbuckling my belt first then undoing the button to my jeans. Her hand plunged down inside my underwear, and I let out a deep breath as my head fell back and she stroked Coltrane firmly. Don't get me wrong this shit was feeling wonderful, but again... I wanted what was in between her legs and not her hands.

"You know what I want, Izzy," I said breathlessly because what she was doing to me felt so damn good. I pulled her hands out of my jeans and turned around to face her. "Give me a kiss," I demanded pulling her into my arms. She lifted up and pressed her lips against mine as my tongue slid inside of her mouth. We continued to make out for a few minutes, but Coltrane was throbbing against my leg.

"How do I get you out of this latex shit?"

"You have to peel me like a banana," Izzy replied playfully. She grabbed at the rubbery material and pulled it off of her skin. She managed to get most of it off her breast, but it was going to take too much time to get her out of that shit.

"I don't have time for this shit," I said and grabbed her crotch. I managed to grip a piece in front of her pelvis and tugged at it. A strange look came across my face because as I pulled a large chunk of it came from her body. I must have looked mortified because Izzy burst into laughter. "What's so funny? This shit is feeling weird as hell."

"It does, but your facial expression is epic!" Izzy called out laughing. I looked at what I had in my hand and it looked like a piece of cloth or something. "You didn't think I'd spread the latex across my pussy, did you? I do have a little respect for myself, and I made sure that I covered my most important part of my body with some fabric. You couldn't tell when you were playing in between my legs at the club? Jack put the latex on thick right there to cover it up."

I looked down at Izzy, and there were pieces of latex sporadically stuck to her skin.

"You know I'm fucked up, but I can't wait to peel all of this shit off of you," I said gripping her ass in my hands. "I'm ready to show out for your birthday and let you know that I was true to this dick game." I rubbed my fingers in between Izzy's legs and the sound of her moan damn near made me nut on myself.

"Wait a minute King," Izzy said breathlessly. "I want to take you somewhere first."

Izzy stepped back away from me grabbing my hand, and we went down a hallway into this dark room toward the back of her condo, and she stopped in front of a door opening it up. I was amazed at what I saw because there were glow in the dark stars and constellations stuck all over the dark colored walls. The night's sky was painted on the ceiling, and the moon along with stars and constellations were in glow in the dark paint. This room was dope, and my high was definitely feeling it.

Izzy walked me over to the bed and pushed me back on it. The muthafucka started to move, and I felt like I was floating. Man, I thought I was tripping and the pills had me gone. This was definitely some different level type shit, but this nigga was with whatever.

"What the fuck is this!" I shouted trying to gain some control. The bed kept hovering in waves, and I couldn't stop myself from moving. "What is going on Izzy? What the fuck am I laying on?"

Izzy just laughed turning on this machine that started making sounds; it was like we were outside or something. "Is that crickets I hear?"

She climbed up on the bed with me and the muthafucka was still in motion.

"It's a waterbed silly. You've never been on one of these before?" Izzy laughed hysterically.

"Hell naw," I replied, laughing uncontrollably. Izzy took off my shoes and started massaging my feet.

"I'm surprised that Sam never had one of these in his house."

"That freaky bastard might have one tucked away in storage, but the real question is why do you have one?"

"This used to be my brother's room," Izzy explained. "He moved away, and I decided to keep the bed because it has secret powers." She slipped her shoes off then climbed up on top of me.

"Not tonight," I said flipping Izzy over on her back. The bed rippled as we both started rocking. "This shit is going to take some getting used to."

"Can you ride the motion of the ocean?" Izzy asked, pulling down both my pants and underwear. Her hands naturally gravitated to my joint, and the magic stroke began slowly.

"I sure can, Miss James," I replied arrogantly before leaning down and kissing her lips. She took her feet and pushed my pants the rest of the way down to my ankles as we continued to tongue each other real raunchy like. My hand moved meticulously in between her legs as my fingers felt her wetness. I pushed two of them deep inside of her with our bodies floating with the motion of the bed.

"I want you inside of me," Izzy moaned urgently against my lips while her hand was still stroking my stiffness. She moved my dick to her center, rubbing it against her folds as I eased all ten inches deeply inside of her sopping wet walls. Pulling back out of her, the bed was rocking with me, and pushing back up in her had it shifting again.

"Put your feet against the side of the frame and use the momentum of the water as you push inside of me," Izzy instructed.

"Okay," fell from my lips nervously. This was all new to me, but I could get used to it. It reminded me of the time I had sex with this girl on a boat down in Mexico. "Aaaahhhhh, Izzy, you feel so damn good," I moaned, digging deeper inside of her. I could feel my dick stretching out Izzy's folds as her warm breath blew on my damp skin. I pulled halfway out of her and just worked the tip. I knew how to satisfy a woman, but the kid wasn't going to be fucking these young chicks like this. Izzy definitely messed with my ego, and that was the problem. Satisfying her wasn't a top priority because at first, my only concern was getting the coochie when I first laid eyes on her. However, after what she did to me in those curtains, my desire was to be on the receiving end of whatever Miss James was dishing out, and I don't plan on giving her up any time soon.

"Turn over and get this pussy hit from the back," I growled in her ear.

"Are you sure you can handle it?" Izzy asked contracting her muscles and making my dick slide out.

"Fuck yeah!" I shouted, smacking her ass when she tooted it up in the air. I rubbed my head against her lips pushing forcefully inside of her. I must have used too much force because my momentum caused us to float further up the bed.

"Damn!" I yelled as Izzy giggled, but Mr. Coltrane didn't fall out of that twat. Izzy pushed back on me, and I pushed her forward as the wild bumpy ride had begun.

Izzy placed one of my hands on her hip to help control my stroke. Her eyes were looking back at me as I jabbed her pussy good, and she kept making this, 'sssss' noise that was steady turning me on. The way her face was frowning up let me know that I was hurting that kitty cat in a good way.

"Give it to me, King," Izzy moaned, and I did what she asked me to do.

I had gotten the hang of this bed, and I was going to have her calling me daddy before it was all over.

My dick continued to pound into her while she played with her clit. The sight of it all in this freaky ass room had my head gone, and I felt like a porn star. My head drifted backward, and my eyes just so happened to look up at the ceiling. There was an oval shape mirror overhead that solidified this experience. "I'm about to cum," Izzy uttered, but I wasn't ready for her to do it yet.

"I don't want you to cum yet, baby," I groaned. "Hold it just a little longer for daddy."

"Oooo… kkkk… kay, King," Izzy stuttered. I pulled back just a little because I knew if I gave it all to her. She was going to let loose before time.

"Move your hand, Izzy," I told her because her fingers were the problem. They were strumming away on her clit, and it made me decided to switch some shit up on her. "Turn over!"

Izzy turned to the side and swung her leg around without me even having to really move a muscle. It was like this chick had rotated on my dick and I damn near lost my mind.

"Shit, Izzy! You gone have a nigga sprung off this good puss puss; your ass is limber as fuck."

Izzy giggled as she stared into my eyes. I leaned down and licked her lips because they were looking so juicy to me, and my body was losing control.

"Make me cum, King… I want to cum all over your big ass dick. Tame this pussy to claim this pussy," Izzy moaned out suggestively.

Is that a challenge? I thought to myself staring intensely into her eyes. This woman must be kidding because I'm going to make her ass fall in love with this 'little boy' as she calls me.

"If I tame her, is she going to be only mine?" I asked, digging deep down into her womb.

Izzy licked her lips and bit the bottom one because the force I was giving her had both pleasure and pain.

"Aaaaaahhhhhh…" was the only thing that she could manage to get out.

"Is this pussy mine, Izzy?" I asked again. "You have to let me know."

Her back arched as her eyes closed, so that let me know she was avoiding the question. I pulled back at the opening of her folds and only fucked her with the head. Her eyes shot opened as Izzy brought her head down staring wearily into my eyes.

"Why are you teasing me? I… I… I want it all," her voice stammered.

"You're a greedy girl, Izzy. You want me to give you all of this dick, but you're not willing to give it all only to me."

"Don't be childish, Kingdom," Izzy whined. "I want it all, and you need to give it to me, now!"

"So demanding, Miss James. You want me to give it all to you?" I asked playfully.

"Yes," she whispered as I pushed a little more inside of her.

"Call me daddy," I demanded, pulling back to where only the head was sexing her. Izzy bit her bottom lip and arched her back trying to use the momentum of the bed to force more of me inside of her, but it didn't work.

I pulled back even more and almost came out of her, but Izzy pushed back down making my entire thing go deep down inside of her. She tightened her walls and started fucking me back and there was nothing that I could do but enjoy it. This bed was a mutha-fucka, and her ass knew exactly how to use it. We stared into each other's eyes and we both moaned passionately before I felt myself about to nut.

"Oh shit, Izzy!" I called out speeding up my pace.

"I'm about to cum," she called out. Then we both came together making my fucking toes curl. I pushed down deeper spilling all of my seed inside of her. She wrapped her legs around my waist and continued to hump me wildly.

"Yes, daddy! Oh, my gosh, King... you're aaaaammm-maaaazzzziiiinnnnggggg!" Izzy yelled. I buried my head in the nape of her neck and continued to stroke her slowly. My head was spent, and I didn't have anything left in me as I collapsed on top of her. We both were trying to catch our breaths, and I could feel the warm air from her mouth against my skin. I rolled over beside her as the bed sent our bodies moving up and down. We didn't say anything for the next twenty minutes, but I knew at that moment that Izzy was going to be mine.

TWENTY-TWO

Izzy

THIS BIRTHDAY WAS for the books. I would have normally gone out with Craig, which his sorry ass called me with a dinner invitation. Uhhh... no, thank you, sir! I'm not interested in nothing that you're serving. However, I am going to keep the Zac Posen dress, the Audemars Piguet watch and the Hermes bag that he had delivered to my office by a singing telegram. He first sent me thirty white roses with four white Calla lilies in a bouquet. I guess that was supposed to make me rush to call his ass to thank him, but instead, I sent the flowers back and told Jack to tell the florist that they had the wrong place. Craig decided to pull out the big guns and give me an actual present.

Maybe it was wrong for me to be acting this way, but that dude had me so messed up that it's ridiculous. He took that wannabe Barbie to Vegas for her birthday, so shitty flowers along with a shitty dinner was not going to cut it this year!

How did I end up with this fine man in my bed last night? I pondered as the weight of his arm rested heavily on my waist? His warm breath felt so good against my skin, and I could definitely get used to this. He showed out at the club buying me all of those bottles, and he definitely redeemed himself with that dick down he gave me last night. It was surprising at how quickly he caught on to the waterbed, and he used that sucker to his advantage. I thought that he got the first round off with the help of bed, but when he got me upstairs in the shower, good lawd I thought I had died and gone to heaven!

I took my wig off and let my real hair down. He washed it along with my body then we got out of the shower and made sweet love so tenderly until the sun came up. That man-child had me calling him daddy repeatedly. I even fell asleep sucking his thumb like a newborn baby. Gosh, fucking a twenty-something may be a good thing, but got damn, I was ashamed of myself. I talked all that shit about him being too young, how he couldn't work his dick, and all the time, this boy was playing me for a fool. Look at his precious ass lying next to me all cuddled up and shit. This dude had the nerve to throw his leg over me so that I couldn't move. Also, he kept talking some stuff about me being his exclusive cut buddy, but I didn't know if I wanted that. His ass was going to have me with a flashlight trying to find him, and I can't do it, especially not at my age, baby. My prime years were approaching, and King was not going to waste any of them. The idea of him being my cut buddy at first seemed like a wonderful idea. However, after what I experienced last night into the early morning, I might fall in love with his ass too soon. He had his whole life ahead of him and didin't need to be tied down to a thirty-something year old woman who couldn't even get an older man to propose to her.

"What are you thinking about?" King whispered in my ear. He placed a wet kiss on my bare shoulder and the hairs on the back of my neck stood up.

"Nothing," I replied, lying to him. "Did you get enough rest?"

"Are you kidding?" he said, chuckling. "We didn't drift off to sleep until a few hours ago."

"That's because someone wanted to tell me their life story," I teased.

"So you got jokes this morning. Say you're sorry," he replied tickling me. I laughed hysterically while I tried to fight him off, but his strength was too much for me.

"I'm sorry," I managed to get out between laughs. "Please stop tickling me, King." But he continued to lay it on thick.

"Say 'please stop, daddy,'" he replied. "Ask daddy to stop tickling you." I continued to laugh hard, and it felt like I was going to pee on myself.

"I'm not playing, King! You're going to make me pee on myself."

"Your nasty ass is the one who's going to have to clean it up," he replied, chuckling. "Now ask daddy to stop. You didn't have any problems calling me daddy last night when I was serving you this dick." That was hitting below the belt, but all is fair in love and war.

"Please stop, daddy," I said with tears in my eyes. I was laughing so hard that my side started to ache. "I want you to stop, King... I mean... daddy."

"That's more like it," he said stopping. He rolled me over and wiped the tears from eyes before leaning down and kissing my lips tenderly. I wrapped my arms around his neck, and he slid in between my legs.

"You remember what you said to me last night, don't you?"

"I was drunk and high off ecstasy, King. I could have said anything to you last night," I replied nervously. I knew what he was talking about, but I tried to play dumb.

"You said, Elizabeth James, that you would consider being my exclusive fuck buddy," King reminded me. "And your ass wasn't that drunk when we talked about it. I know that you have reservations about messing with a younger man. We talked about that in depth last night as well, but no one has to know what's going on between us two consenting adults." He kissed my lips then my neck and licked my nipple with his tongue. "You know you like me inside of you, Izzy James, so stop being so stubborn and submit to me." He stared at me with those gorgeous eyes, and my heart melted inside of my chest.

"How can I resist those beautiful eyes?" I kissed his lips softly. "Those big pink juicy lips and... That great big anaconda you have in between your legs!" I yelled. "Oh my! You got me feeling so conflicted."

"Why Izzy?" he questioned. "You know this feels so right. I'm not going to take no for an answer, so you better tell Craig and any other nigga that's sniffing at your skirt that they better step the fuck off because your pussy belongs to me now."

"But I thought we were going to be fuck buddies."

"We are," he replied smugly. "But we're excluuuuusive fuck buddies," he clarified.

"Well, if that's the case, then you can't be going around screwing all those young and old thots that you and Sam be picking up at the clubs," I countered. "And that counselor at the university can't get none of the goods either." King furrowed his brow and stared at me for a second.

"Wait… how did you know about Sarah?" he asked.

"Who's Sarah?" I asked in response and sat up in the bed. King moved over to the side of me and sat back against the headboard.

"I asked you first," he replied. "I mean how do you even know I was screwing my counselor at the university?"

I decided to come clean and tell him that I overheard Duchess and Chelsea talking about it. I let him know that Chelsea was the one who brought it to his mother's attention. I went on to tell him that his mother doesn't want me or any other older woman messing with her son and that it seemed like Duchess had plans on hooking him and Chelsea up.

"Look, King, I'm not going to lie to you. I think you're a wonderful young man, and I thoroughly enjoy having sex with you. However, if we continue on this path, I'm afraid that I might fall in love with you, and I couldn't stand it if you didn't feel the same way that I do or even break my heart for that matter."

King moved the hair out of my face before he kissed my lips. My mouth welcomed his tongue hungrily as we continued kissing nastily. He pulled me up onto his lap inserting himself inside of me. I gasped against his lips from his thickness filling me up as my forehead pressed against his.

"I want all of you, Izzy. I want your mind, body, and soul," King said in a serious tone.

"Don't say it if you don't mean it, King," I whispered while he kept lifting up inside of me.

"I want to grow to love you, Izzy. I don't care if you're older than I am. Age doesn't mean a thing to me," he insisted. "Let me learn you, Izzy James. Show me how to take care of you like you showed me how to fuck you."

I pressed my lips against King's to stop his words. My body started shaking because this was too good to be true. Please, God, wake me up. This has to be a dream.

King broke away and planted kisses all around my neck and shoulders. He continued to pump deep inside of me while I rocked my hips back and forth.

"Cum for me, baby. I want you to release your juices all over this dick... your dick, Izzy," he whispered in my ear.

"Sssshhhhh," I said, trying to concentrate because his words were making me intoxicated. "Stop, Kingdom. Please stop saying those things to me if you don't mean them."

"But I mean them," he replied. "Give yourself to me, Izzy. We can take small steps if that's what you want."

We stared into each other's eyes as I felt myself about to climax, and when he took my nipple into his mouth sucking on it forcefully, I came so hard that my body shook in his arms.

"See... can't nobody make you cum like me," King uttered triumphantly. He continued humping inside of me, and my body fell limp on his chest. He turned me over on my back and continued to go deeper and deeper inside of me.

"I want you to make daddy cum."

"Yes sir. Give it all to me," I whispered for some strange reason. Oh no! I'm starting to get dickmatized already. "Cum for me, King."

"What's my name?" he demanded, pounding hard into my walls. "What's my name, Izzy?"

"Daaaaddy... uhhh... uhhhh... daddy," came uttering from my lips breathlessly.

That must have sent his ass over the edge because his pace quickened, and my walls felt his dick contract inside of me.

"Ohhhhh shit, Izzy!" King yelled out as he released himself inside of me. He looked down at me smiling that boyish grin, and I couldn't help but smile back because this dude already had my heart, and he didn't even know it.

"Let's go take a shower," I said before kissing his lips. "But we're not having sex in there."

"We'll see about that, Izzy," King replied, laughing.

KING and I were sitting at my kitchen table eating lunch. We were feeding each other fresh fruit off of the fruit tray that I had bought from the farmer's market. We were so smitten by each other, and the feeling was unbelievable. King kept stealing kisses, which in turn had me giggling like a little girl. I loved the way he made me feel, and it was intoxicating. I didn't want this time to end, but soon reality would set in and we would have to go our separate ways.

"Since your birthday was yesterday and I didn't know it, I feel the need to make it up to you," King said, feeding me a piece of pineapple.

"First of all, you didn't know, and I think the way you've been sexing me is the best present that you could give me," I replied. He looked at me as if he were offended.

"Izzy, I don't want you to think of me for only that," King snapped. "There is more to me than just my ten inches of Grade A dick."

"I'm sorry, King. I didn't mean to offend you. However, we're only supposed to be cut buddies, remember?"

"Well, you did… and another thing," he said, frowning. I stared at him with a surprised look on my face. "I'm going to show you how sincere I am about being with you."

"Not if you're going to get an attitude whenever I make a comment about your enormous penis," I replied in a stank tone of voice. King raised an eyebrow at me, so I raised one of mine up too. A slight smile played on his lips and I stared his ass down like a professional. "Let's get one thing straight, young man. You will not raise your voice at me, especially not up in my shit. Now I said your ass don't have to do anything else for me, so you can either take it or leave it because I really don't give a fuck." King looked at me in shock and put his fork down. He pushed away from the table, and before I knew it, he had grabbed me up out of my chair and put me in his lap.

"I am so turned on right now," he said, laughing. He tickled me on my stomach and I began to laugh hysterically. He stopped, wrapping his arms around my waist and kissing my lips tenderly. "You are something else Izzy, but I'm going to wear your ass down."

"I don't know about that youngster, but you can try," I replied. My phone case lit up, so I knew it was about to ring. "Shit! I guess it was too good to be true." I went to reach for it and King grabbed my hand.

"Don't answer it," he said. "Just sit here with me and let's enjoy our lunch."

"As much as I want to, babe, I have to answer my phone. It's a part of my job, and I'm always on call," I explained. Lifting up, I grabbed my phone off the table. "Hello. Izzy James speaking."

"Hi, Izzy," Jack said cheerfully. "How was last night?" I looked at King and smiled.

"Wonderful. What's up?"

"I have some good news and some bad news, so which one do you want first?" Jack asked.

"Give me the bad news first," I replied nestling into King's arms.

"Well the clueless wonder has struck again," Jack replied. "She didn't get the garment bags packed to be delivered this morning, and a certain celebrity did not get her outfit for the luncheon today."

"Shit! That little dumb ass cunt!" came roaring out of my mouth.

"Yes, she is," Jack agreed. "However, the good news is that certain celebrity wasn't mad because she had something in her closet to wear, but she said you're going to have to dress her for free in two weeks for some Thanksgiving Gala that she has to attend for the homeless."

"What's the matter, baby?" King asked concerned. "Is everything all right?"

"Is that Kingdom's voice I hear?" Jack asked nosily. "It's one o'clock in the afternoon and he's still at your house?"

"Yes nosy," I replied smugly, pushing the mute button on the phone and smiling at King warmly. "Everything is fine. I'm going to go take this call in the other room."

Getting up off King's lap, we gave each other a wet kiss. I walked out of the kitchen heading toward the living room because I didn't want King to hear me answering Jack's questions.

"Hello."

"Did your ass mute the phone bitch?" Jack asked with an attitude.

"Yes, I did, bitch," I replied smugly. "I was sitting on his lap and he could hear every word that your big mouth ass said."

"Oooohhhh," Jack replied. "I guess you must have enjoyed that little number. That's cute."

"You mean that big member," I replied laughing. I looked back in the kitchen at King and he was looking at his phone. "He's got me turned the fuck out, and I don't know what I'm going to do."

"I know one thing, you better not run, bitch!" Jack yelled. "If his ass didn't get the fuck up and leave last night after y'all had sex or left this morning before breakfast, then guurrlll… his ass is not going anywhere no time soon."

"You think?" I uttered biting down on my bottom lip. "I mean, I don't want him to leave, but I can't get wrapped up in this madness. Maybe he's just being polite."

"Or maybe he really likes you, bitch! Get your head out of your ass and accept whatever he's trying to give you!"

"You better stop yelling at me, Jack," I snapped. "Don't forget who's the oldest person on this phone!"

"Stop being stupid, Izzy, because you're really getting on my nerves," Jack scoffed. "I guess you want that tired muthafucka Craig to come over, huh?"

"No, I don't want to see his ass. Didn't I blow him off yesterday?"

"Yes, you did, and I'm proud of you," Jack insisted. "However, I want you to be accepting of the gift that's right in front of you, and I hope you get injured while slutting yourself out to him."

King came out of the kitchen walking up on me. He wrapped his arms around my waist, kissing my cheek softly.

"I need to head home to grab some clothes," King said, rocking us back and forth. "But when I come back, I'm going to take you somewhere nice because it's still your birthday." He planted kisses on my neck, and I melted in his arm.

"Okay, babe. But I need to go to the office for a while. My dumb ass intern messed up again, and I have to go straighten things out."

"Can't Jack take care of it?" King asked bringing his hands up and pinching my nipples. My butt instantly pushed back into him as my eyes closed.

"He could take care of it, but it's my name on the business cards, so I have to go do this myself. How about I catch an Uber to the studio and you can come pick me up when I'm done."

"That sounds like a plan," King replied still toying with my breast. "I'm about to go upstairs and put on my clothes. I expect you to be off the phone when I come back downstairs so that you can send me off properly."

Jack started talking shit in my ear, so I hung up on him. Turning to face King, my reply was simple, "See, it's done."

TWENTY-THREE

King

DAMN, that woman had my head gone. I couldn't believe the shit that was coming out of my mouth to Izzy, but I meant every word of it. She's intelligent, beautiful, successful, and her pussy was good as hell. What more was there to love about her? I think it was divine intervention that we ended up at the same club where Izzy was celebrating her birthday. My ego was happy that Coltrane was able to redeem himself by laying this pipe down properly. I had her calling me daddy by the end of the night, and she even promised to give a relationship with me a try. Well, it's a fuck buddy relationship, but I intended on turning it into something more.

I pulled up to Pops house, and I noticed his car was parked out front. Punching the code into the keypad, I waited for the gate to open. We hadn't talked in two weeks because I avoided his calls too. It seemed like I was acting like a bitch ass nigga, but my Pops tried to play me. He should have told Izzy to address her thoughts to me instead of listening and telling me that we needed to talk about some things.

Going into the house, my first thought was to go into the kitchen. I figured Pops was probably in the family room watching television, so it would be easier to grab me something to drink, get my clothes, and duck out to go pick up Izzy. I was thinking about taking her somewhere overnight, and we could spend time getting to know one another.

Pops was sitting at the kitchen table reading the newspaper. He pulled it down and looked at me as I walked over to the refrigerator. Grabbing the handle and opening it up, I took a fruit juice off the shelf then closed it.

"King, I know you're not going to walk up in my house and disrespect me," Pops said sternly.

"My fault, Pops. What's up?" I replied dryly.

"I know you're not still mad about that Izzy situation."

"No, sir. I'm not even tripping off that anymore," I replied. "She explained to me what happened, and I'm over it. However, I would like for you to know that your grandson was able to get up on Izzy again, and I knocked the boots up off that putang!"

"Boy! Your ass didn't do shit," Pops scoffed, laughing. He put his newspaper back up and went back to reading it. "I want to apologize to you for what happened, King. I should have handled the situation differently, but I was so excited to see that you were able to hook Izzy, and when she said that you didn't know how to handle your dick, well, my pride and ego got the best of me." Pops folded up the paper, placing it down on the table. He was looking at me sternly, and I saw my future self-staring back at me.

"I guess that was a blow to your ego, Pops. You did spend a lot of money on my sex life and you knew the women you paid taught me well."

"You damn right!" Pops spat. "Them hoes used to do me good, so I know they were knocking you down properly. That's high-priced pussy my money paid for. You had to pay at least a thousand dollars or better to even get any of those hoes to get out of their beds." I laughed at my grandfather because he had a way with words. "It was Sylvia who turned you into a man, and she was the best that money could buy. Sylvia had movie stars, singers, and professional athletes paying for that poo-nanny, and I got her special for you, grandson."

"Man, that broad had a body on her, and she rode me all

night," I recalled. "Sylvia told me that I had too much dick for a sixteen-year-old, and my mama better keep an eye on me." We both laughed, and I watched my grandfather's eyes twinkle.

"Let me ask you a question Pops."

"What's up, King?" he asked before taking a sip out of his coffee cup.

"Have you ever had sex on a waterbed before?" I asked curiously.

"What you know about that, King?" Pops asked with a curious look on his face. "I got one of those at my house up in Colorado. They can be a lot of fun."

"I know," I replied smiling. "Izzy's brother left one at her house and we screwed on it last night. It was Izzy's birthday, so this good dick was a part of her present."

"That's right… Izzy is a Scorpio," Pops recalled. "You better watch yourself. That girl's a professional freak. A woman her age shouldn't know anything about a waterbed." I laughed at him because that was insane to me. "You're laughing, but I'm telling you the truth. You know what Tyrese said about Scorpios, 'she has no limits to where she'll go', boy!"

"Pops, you're wild as a mug. I can't believe you're quoting song lyrics to me." My head shook back and forth in disbelief. "But you do have a vast knowledge in freakism." Pops laughed at my comment.

"I was listening to that song last night when I was on my way downtown," Pops said getting up from his chair. "How did you end up with Izzy?"

"I was on Hollywood Boulevard with my boys, and we ran into her at a club," I explained. I went into my phone and pulled up a picture of her from last night at the club. I held it out in front of my grandfather, and his eyes narrowed at the photo.

"What does she have on? It looks like she's ass naked," Pops scoffed.

"She was naked and painted with latex, but I enjoyed peeling it off her ass. It felt like her body was covered with a condom."

"I tell you that girl is something else," Pops said, laughing. "I remember one year we went to Vegas for her birthday. She and her friend Ash dressed up like the Playboy Bunnies, and they got so many compliments on their costumes."

"You know a lot about my woman. Where do you think would be a good place to take Izzy for her birthday? I want to impress her, but I want us to have some privacy."

"Are you okay, grandson?" Pops asked. "You're showing some genuine interest in Izzy, and I'm confused."

"Huh…" I uttered. "What are you talking about?"

"I thought you weren't interested in no chicks. You said all you're going to do is screw them and move on to the next one," Pops explained. "We're supposed to be 'Casanovas… eligible bachelors' per your words."

I laughed at Pops because he was trying to drive me. Those were my feelings before I spent the night with Izzy. However, now getting to know her better is my top priority because there's something about Elizabeth James that has piqued my curiosity.

"I know what was said, Pops, but Izzy's different. I've always liked older women because that's what you exposed me to. Besides, Izzy and I are just getting to know each other, and things are on a touch and go basis right now."

Pops looked at me and laughed. He wasn't buying the shit, and I wasn't either. Izzy had a brother going, and I couldn't wait to see her later.

"Didn't you say that you wanted to do something special for her?" Pops asked inquisitively.

"Yeah. She turned thirty-four yesterday, and I wanted to do something real special for her. I could take her to an expensive restaurant, but Izzy mentioned that Jack her assistant took her out to dinner last night. I thought about taking her to Six Flags, but then that would be a bit juvenile, don't you think?"

"Definitely, but you should save that date for another time," Pops replied. "Izzy seems like the type who would enjoy a date like that, but you don't want to take her there for her birthday. You want to leave a lasting impression and do something that's going to have her thinking about it for weeks. Something that will have her eating out of the palm of your hands."

"I'm with it Pops, but what does that look like?" I asked, leaning against the counter. Staring out of the window I noticed a car parked on the side of the gate.

"Did you know there's a car parked on the side of the gate?"

"Yeah, but it's all good," Pops replied. "That's Peter, and he's watching the house from the outside."

"Why? Is something wrong?" I asked concerned.

"There's nothing to be concerned about, but this chick I was messing with had followed me here. You know my rule about bringing women to this house, and she thought that Gail our house-keeper was my woman."

"Seriously?"

"Seriously! She tried to climb the gate to get in, and I saw her entire meltdown on the security tape, so as an extra precaution Peter is sitting out there while we're at the house," Pops explained. I looked at him questionably because that didn't sound right to me. Pops has been in the streets for decades, and he's never been worried about no woman.

"I'm about to go take a shower and think about what I want to do with Izzy. Weren't you the one who told me that you can't sex every woman the same?"

"Yes, I did," Pops replied.

"So, how do you know when it's appropriate to bang a chick or finesse that ass?" I asked curiously. "Because I just bang all of them."

"And that's why Izzy said you don't know what to do with all of that dick," Pops joked, laughing. "King, when I told you that, you were sixteen years old. The next time I mentioned it you were eigh-teen and out here having fun. I would have hoped that you learned the difference in seeking out how to pleasure a woman. It's not all about ramming your hard-on into a woman and leaving her tired and sore afterward. It's about making sure the experience is good for the both of you and not you getting off a nut."

"I'm telling you, Pops, these chicks love a good pounding," I said, hunching my shoulders. "But I do recognize that Izzy is different, and tonight, I'm going to finesse that ass, making her forget about my age again and again and again."

———————

A HOT SHOWER was definitely what a brother needed. I had my music beating through the house, and I was amped about going to get Izzy. I still hadn't figured out what we were doing, but as long as I got to hang out with her it didn't matter what we did. I had just put on my pants on when I heard a knock at the door.

"King! I got something for you," said Pops through the door.

"Okay!" I yelled over the music. Walking over to the radio, I turned it off before going to open the door. "What's up, Pops?"

"I figured out what you can do for Izzy's birthday," he said walking into my room. "I've already made the arrangements and all you have to do is go get her."

"Oh yeah? What's the play?"

"I made you a reservation at Rancho Valencia in Southern California. It's a short drive there, and it's romantic as hell. I used to take a special friend of mine there all of the time and we always had a wonderful time," Pops explained. "The suite is booked for two nights, and you can come back on Monday. You guys got the best spa package that they offer and the room you're staying in will have Izzy eating out the palm of your hand."

"Thanks, Pops! I appreciate it."

"I know you do, King," Pops replied. "KiKi said that she's taken care of the payment arrangements, so when you see the charge on your monthly statement you'll know where it came from."

"Damn! I thought you were going to pay for it since you made the reservation," I scoffed with a smirk on my face.

"Nigga, please! Your ass is worth millions. What the hell I look like paying for a trip for you and your new boo?" Pops replied, chuckling. "However, you can use my jet if you don't want to drive, and you won't be charged for it."

"Bet! Thank you for all of your help Pops. I only wish that my father put as much interest into me as you do."

"I talked to Duchess yesterday, and she said that Chester was gone out of town for a few weeks," Pops said nonchalantly. "I think you shouldn't worry about that, King, because if Chester can't recognize how special you are then that's his loss."

"It is his loss, but it's still unfortunate for the both of us."

IZZY CALLED to let me know that she was ready to go. I told her to pack a small bag because we were going on an overnight trip. She tried to give me trouble, but I shut her ass down with the quickness, assuring her that my understanding about her running a business was dutifully noted. However, it was her birthday, and she needed to let Jack handle things because that's what personal assistants are for.

Jack agreed with me while shouting insults in the background, making Izzy take me off of speakerphone. Finally, she agreed to go along with what I had planned which made me so excited about taking her on this trip. Izzy was going to get pampered, spoiled and sexed so good that she wasn't going to want to leave at the end of the trip.

Pulling up the studio, I called to tell her to come out. I didn't want to go inside because I knew Jack would make a scene. It was already known that he was extra and over the top. My nerves could only put up with so much of that gay shit, but I might as well get used to it because Miss James was going to be mine.

I got out of my car and leaned against the passenger door waiting for Izzy to come out. I had on a white V-neck Polo t-shirt with a pair of tan cargo pants, a thick off-white Ralph Lauren cable knit button-up sweater and a pair of leather slides because I'm a Californian and shoes are always optional.

I stopped at the barbershop and got my face shaved to look sexy for my baby because thoughts of her complaining about my stubble scratching her skin jumped into my head.

Izzy walked out of the door with a big smile spread across her face. The long loose-fitting burgundy cotton dress that draped her body looked sexy as hell. Then the way her long olive green hooded sweater jacket hugged her hips made me wonder if all of her clothes were painted on. She had on a pair of olive green wedges that showed her pretty manicured toes, and her hair was pulled up into a messy bun with a few tendrils of hair coming down on the sides. Izzy's hair was black with blonde streaks, but the red sew-in she had when we first met really turned me on.

I stared lustfully at her as she approached me. We shared a kiss before I gave her the single red rose that I was holding, and her eyes lit up even more. This felt so right in this moment that there's no way this wasn't destiny.\

"For me?" Izzy asked coyly.

"For you," I replied, leaning down kissing her lips softly. Her hand touched my cheek as we continued to kiss, and I could hear comments coming from the peanut gallery. It was mainly Jack, and Izzy pulled away laughing while wiping her lip gloss off of my lips.

"I'm ready to go, babe," Izzy said bashfully as I took her bag out of her hand. "Where is this place you're taking me?"

"It's a surprise," I replied opening Izzy's door and helping her inside. I proceeded to put her bag in the trunk and she leaned over to open my door. A big smile appeared on my face because that means my baby is really a keeper with her old school ass.

"Thanks," I said getting into the car. I picked up her hand and kissed the back of it because I knew I was going to enjoy this trip. Izzy was looking beautiful and relaxed and I was feeling good. There was nothing that could mess up this day and I refused to let anything do it.

"Fire up that joint that's in that tube," I instructed Izzy. "I stopped at the dispensary before I came here and grabbed a few goodies."

"A man after my own heart," Izzy gushed. "I bought a few buds too, so I guess we're going to be good and high this trip." I looked over at her smiling.

"I still feel that demo we took last night, so I'm riding on semi," I replied.

"I still feel that ecstasy too, and it has my body feeling wonderful," Izzy acknowledged. I looked over at her and lifted my eyebrows.

"This good dick I gave you last night has you feeling wonderful. Please don't get the two confused," I said arrogantly. Izzy giggled and hit me on the arm. I reached my hand over and tickled under her chin, but she leaned it down on my hand to stop me from making her laugh. "You have the most beautiful smile Izzy, and I love that giggle of yours."

"It sounds like somebody's got a crush," Izzy teased. "However, I'm sort of crushing on you, too." I licked my lips and bobbed my head to the music because Usher's "Can You Handle It" was doing all of the talking for me.

We rode down the Interstate 110 in silence because there was nothing left to say for the moment. We both kept stealing glances at one another and Izzy took my hand in hers and placed it on her lap. I could tell that she was a bit nervous, but so was I. I had never done anything like this before, and it was like she was popping my cherry.

"Why are we pulling up at an airport?" Izzy asked curiously.

"Because we're about to take a short plane ride. My Pops loaned me his jet, and I'm about to whisk you away for two days. Is that cool with you?"

"That's cool with me," Izzy replied before leaning over and kissing my lips tenderly. This was going to be a trip for the books.

TWENTY-FOUR

Izzy

_____

KING WAS PULLING out all of the stops. Being whisked away on a private jet to an undisclosed destination screams romantic to me. Maybe I underestimated this young man. He seemed to be stepping up to the plate and putting his intentions out there. It was hard for me to take him seriously because a lot of young men's attention span is as short as the days are long. How many times have you experienced a man juggling several women and he can barely manage the main one he's trying to hold on to? I don't want to feed too much into this because maybe this is just a nice gesture he's doing for my birthday.

"Let me ask you a question, King. How many women have you whisked away on a private jet?"

"To be honest with you, Izzy. You're the first woman that I've ever done this with," King replied shyly. "Most of the trips that I've taken have been with my family. When Pops and I travel, we normally meet new women where we are, or he has them meet us there." My eyes narrowed at him and a smile spread across his face.

"Why do I find that hard to believe? I mean, the great Kingdom McDaniel has never taken a woman on a trip," I teased him.

"Nope. I've never taken a woman on a trip like this. I guess you're popping my cherry," King said walking toward me. He leaned down and kissed my lips then presented me with a glass of champagne. We were up in the air, and the pilot said we'd be at our destination in a little over an hour.

Taking the glass out of his hand, we stared at each other intently. King hit his glass against mine then we took a sip at the same time. Next, he took my glass out of my hand and set both of them over on a table across the aisle from us. He had this seductive look on his face, and I could tell that he was up to something.

"Have you ever been introduced to the mile-high club?" I asked suggestively.

"Only once when Pops and I ran these two stewardesses when we were on our way to New York. We had gotten so drunk, and the women were very familiar with Pops," King explained, laughing. "But I don't want to talk about that right now. What I want to do is something we haven't ventured into yet."

"And what is that?"

"You'll see in a second, so relax, baby. You're going to enjoy it," King cooed.

King took me by the hand and pulled me up to my feet. He stared into my eyes as he bent down, lifting the bottom of my dress up over my hips. I was sliding my arms out of my jacket while he rubbed his hands up my thighs, grabbing the sides of my thong. My legs parted some because being accommodating shows good manners and there's no need for a struggle.

"Can I taste you, Izzy?" King cooed at me.

"It depends," I said, running my hands through his dreads and grabbing a few, wrapping them around my hands. "Kiss her," uttered from my lips as my hand tugged on his hair.

"Yes ma'am," King replied respectfully, leaning in for a kiss. He licked his tongue out and I pulled his hair again looking at him displeased.

"Your instructions were to kiss her, sir. Please do what is asked of you," I sternly advised. King looked up at me with a glimmer in his eyes then he leaned forward and kissed my sweet spot. "Good boy... now proceed."

"With pleasure."

King licked my folds and my body shivered as his tongue flickered against my clit. Lifting my leg, he placed it on his shoulder as he pushed his face further into my goodness. My head automatically fell back as King's stiff tongue went deep inside of me.

"That's it, babe. Taste the rainbow," I cooed humping his face. King had his arm positioned up under my leg as his hand supported my back. His tongue swiped down my folds, latching back onto my money spot.

"Oooohhhh, King, your tongue feels so good. Make mommy cum."

"Hhhmmm..." King moaned against my spot. He pushed two fingers inside of my wetness, making my knees give out. "Gotcha," King said, catching me before I hit the floor. He placed me in the seat, lifting my legs up in the air. He spread them apart, licking my clit, and I purred like a kitten as he pleasured me so good. My core started to tingle, and my legs shook as my orgasm rose up through my body.

"Yes, baby," I whined. "Yes King, baby... yes!" My orgasm shot through my body like a rocket with my legs trembling uncontrollably against his face. My hands grabbed ahold of his dreads, pulling them like a horse's reign. "Good boy... oh gosh! Good boy."

King rose up with my juices all over his face, and he leaned in to kiss my lips. My tongue licked his top lip before his mouth engulfed mine. I welcomed his tongue hungrily as we kissed nastily. If this little demonstration was a sample of what's to come, then bring it on, Mr. Kingdom McDaniel, because I was ready to receive all of this good loving.

TWENTY-FIVE

Chelsea

I WAS out running errands for Duchess, and the last one of the day involved me taking Izzy James a thank you gift. Duchess was so pleased with the photoshoot, even though she tried her best to sabotage it. She can do the most sometimes, and some of the stuff Duchess was complaining about didn't make sense. I especially liked the way Izzy handled her because she wasn't going to let Duchess mess up her plans at all.

King looked so fire in his suit, and when Izzy put that crown on his head, I wanted to bow down in front of him and give him the best head of his life. However, I needed to concentrate on dropping this package off and lusting after King's ass could come later.

The navigation got me to Izzy's street, and I felt relieved because I hated being lost. Everyone knew that Downtown LA can be a bit sketchy in some areas, and the last thing I needed was a homeless person running up to my car.

Continuing down the street, I spotted the studio on the right-hand side. It looked like King's Porsche was sitting in the parking lot, but why would he be at Izzy's shop? The further I drove toward the place, I could see that my suspicions were correct. King got out of his car and walked around to the passenger side. He leaned against the car, then Izzy came out carrying some type of bag.

I pulled over two cars back and watched as Izzy walked into his arms. They shared a very passionate kiss, and I damn near pulled out of my parking spot and swerved up on King's ass! I just had King's dick in my mouth a week ago and he didn't kiss me like that. When I tried to bring my lips close to his face, he turned his head and told me that he doesn't kiss. Well, I sure as hell couldn't tell 'cause he was surely kissing that bitch! However, I got something for that ass, and I promise he was going to pay for it. I'd been calling and texting him, leaving messages on his phone, in his DM, and messenger, but his response had been nonexistent, and I couldn't believe this shit!

Pulling out my phone, my finger hit the video icon. I taped all of their PDA and decided to follow them to see where they were headed. I wanted to get some more ammo because I intended to show this shit to Duchess. She was going to flip her muthafuckin' lid when she found out that this old ass bitch was fucking her son.

King turned the corner and pulled up to the gate at one of the private airports just outside of LA. I felt myself getting angrier because I couldn't believe he was taking this bitch on a trip. They couldn't have been messing around that long, so why was she getting all of the special treatment? I'd never heard Duchess mention anything about him ever having a girlfriend, and I'd never seen him hanging out with any girl on campus or at his parents' house as a matter fact.

I pulled up to the gate recording him help Izzy out of the car. They shared another kiss, and I almost threw up in my mouth because I felt so sick to my stomach. I had just done King's laundry and put it on his bed with a little note letting him know that I was available to him. I knew he was satisfied with my sexual perfor-mance because I took all of that dick and didn't flinch.

I continued watching and recording this nonsense up until they boarded the plane. I was so enraged by King's betrayal that I couldn't wait to show Duchess my videos.

Uploading them into two separate text messages, I sent that shit to his mama's phone. I couldn't wait for that phone call because she was going to be livid. I knew that Duchess was going to break that shit up before it even got too serious, and I'd be there to pick up all the pieces.

To Be Continued!

Text ROYALTY to 42828 to join our mailing list!

Acknowledgments

I would like to Thank God for giving me this gift of writing. It is a blessing to be able to share my stories with you guys, and I appreciate each and every one of you that come along on my adventures! This book is different from what I've written in the past, and I've enjoyed pushing myself to create this wonderful love story. I would like to thank my publisher, Porscha Sterling, for believing in me and giving me the opportunity to put my thoughts out here in the world! I am truly grateful to you and the Royalty Publishing House family for all of your love and support! I would like to give a special shout out to Quiana Nicole and Michelle Davis for all of their help and support!! I've come to understand that you guys are a major gear in this crazy machine that keeps us shining, and I want you to know that I appreciate y'all! (XoXo) I can't forget my *awesome* editor, Latisha Smith Burns, and her editing team at Touch of Class Publishing Services: "Where class meets perfection!" You are truly a gem, and I appreciate all of the love and support that you give me! You get my oddness, and I am so grateful that you do!! To my test reader, LaShonda "Shawny" Jennings, thank you for your input and realness! You give me my reality check, and I appreciate the love and support! I would like to thank Tam Jernigan for test reading this book for me and giving me the raw truth. I appreciate you for pushing me to write my story and not hold back! I am thankful to all of my readers for being a part of my literary career because you keep me hopeful, humble, and hungry to give you my very best work! To my readers, thank you! Thank you! Thank you! You guys are rock stars, and I am truly grateful to you! You're the real MVP's!

Peace, love, and blessings!
Vivian Blue

Check me out on Social Media

Facebook: Vivian Blue
Instagram: Authorvivianblue
Twitter: @VivBlueAuthor
My website: http://www.Vivianblueauthor.com
Amazon Author's Page:
http://www.amzn.com/-/e/B0177JADR6
Facebook Likes Page:
http://www.Facebook.com/Vivian-Blue-3889021813110701

Also by Vivian Blue

Royalty Publishing House is now accepting manuscripts from aspiring or experienced urban romance authors!

WHAT MAY PLACE YOU ABOVE THE REST:

Heroes who are the ultimate book bae: strong-willed, maybe a little rough around the edges but willing to risk it all for the woman he loves.

Heroines who are the ultimate match: the girl next door type, not perfect - has her faults but is still a decent person. One who is willing to risk it all for the man she loves.

The rest is up to you! Just be creative, think out of the box, keep it sexy and intriguing!

If you'd like to join the Royal family, send us the first 15K words (60 pages) of your completed manuscript to submissions@royaltypublishinghouse.com

Like Our Page!

Be sure to <u>LIKE</u> our Royalty Publishing House page on Facebook!

0580755525

KNAPP BRANCH LIBRARY
13330 CONANT
DETROIT, MICHIGAN 48212
(313) 481-1772

CPSIA information can be obtained
at www.ICGtesting.com
Printed in the USA
LVHW012148081118
596444LV00017B/372/P

9 781717 132185